T0147479

Direct Link

Direct Link

Andrea L. Bartlett

iUniverse, Inc.
New York   Bloomington

iUniverse books may be ordered through booksellers or by contacting:

iUniverse
1663 Liberty Drive
Bloomington, IN 47403
www.iuniverse.com
1-800-Authors (1-800-288-4677)

ISBN: 978-1-4401-5035-7 (sc)
ISBN: 978-1-4401-5037-1 (ebook)

Printed in the United States of America

iUniverse rev. date: 06/03/2009

Dedication

In retrospect, this was probably the hardest page in the book to write. I am blessed with so many friends and family members that it was hard to include only a few.

The first person I would like to thank is my husband, Garry Bullard. His support has helped tremendously, not only for the struggles in creating my characters, but also for the support during the trials in the last year of my life. Never losing faith in what I could do, he kept me grounded. He has made the best situation out of all the difficulties we have faced together. He is my number one fan and the only critic I listen to. I love him and I am proud to call him mine.

The second two people who I owe my gratitude are my precious boys, Wyatt and Ethan Bartlett. They give me strength to do what I love to do, write. Unknowing to them, I am inspired to create because of the happiness they bring. Watching the two grow and seeing their love for each other is indescribable, but that same love provides me with visions for scenes in my books. A parent's joy is immeasurable and they fill me with so much of it. Thank you babies!

I want to thank my friends and of course there are just too many to name. But I want each and every one of you to know; it was because of your patience and listening ears that I was persuaded to finish my second novel.

And like my friends, I thank my family. The ones who overlook their own faults and see too beyond mine, I thank you. I enjoyed writing this book and hope that same joy can be shared reading it!

CHAPTER ONE

APPEARING OUT OF NOWHERE, WEARING HIS Gucci suit tailored to fit his well groomed body and his brown leather, sack style brief case hanging from his strong shoulders, Hank O'Donnell moved through the courthouse, owning the halls with his arrogant stride. He had an assuring walk and promising smile, not yet tainted and aged by the battles and defeat of the justice system.

An exquisite individual and no stranger to the women in the small Texas City, his thrilling and enchanting character, almost magical, left woman groveling from his boyish good looks. Hank possessed more style and chic than ten men his age. Not only was he something sweet to look at, his ability to play the part was worth an Oscar. Women of all professions, young and old would stop just to say hello, including Jill.

Jill Holland followed her dream of becoming a lawyer and had spent the last two years with the Lubbock County District Attorney's Office. Pulling herself from the wreckage life had dealt her; she proudly graduated Texas Tech University Law School, walking through her thirties with a little more class.

Leaving the position as criminal investigator, she now worked as an assistant district attorney, ingeniously crafting prosecutorial arguments and manipulating the system to work against the presumed guilty. Five days a week she intimidated the defense attorneys and put together sensational cases to influence the juries.

As she cleaned up the hallway, she remembered the first time she had witnessed the new public defender in action, working to acquit his client of all charges, and never abandoning his cause. She was impressed with Hank's integrity to see beyond the criminal, to look further into the accusations revolving around those he was defending and forcing the District Attorney's Office to double check their work.

She struggled to catch her breath after the young attorney rushed directly into her, leaving the courtroom following a modification hearing. His mere presence made her body shiver and her face flush. Kneeling on the cold tile, his broad body followed her to the floor. As she scuffled to pick up the mess he had caused knocking her folders out of her arms, she could smell his cologne empty into her lungs. Watching his hands gather loose papers, Jill noticed he wasn't wearing a wedding band.

"Are you alright?" There was nothing in his voice that made her believe he wasn't genuinely interested. His tone was deep, but smooth and tender to her ears.

Jill allured Hank's attention. Her auburn hair fell loosely down her back. Her eyes were a deep shade of green and her lips were a faint polish of rose. Her skin grinned with a sense of happiness, a touch of warmth, yet not to be covered up with any make-up, just a natural shade of woman.

Standing no taller than five foot four, Hank was taken by her tiny frame and enormous confidence. Jill had a reputation for being stern, but respectful, and Hank had seen it first hand. Weeks earlier, during a pretrial arraignment, Jill stood firm when her team was adamant about seeking a larger bond. He remembered her feisty attitude and imperishable resistance. Hank could see that she cared more about the way she did her job than the way others thought her job should be done. She was strong and confident. Now as they both hurried to clean up the hallway, he could see a hint of fragility seeping with embarrassment, a quality he hadn't expected.

"Do you always knock down everything in your path?" Both lawyers laughed as she swiped a strand of hair behind her ear.

"I'm so sorry," again he smiled and handed her what was left of the papers that had fallen from the folders.

"Don't worry about it." She held out her hand and introduced herself, "I'm Jill Holland. I don't think we've actually met."

Grasping her hand he responded, "Hi, I'm Hank O'Donnell. It is nice to meet you."

He would have loved to stay and hold her hand a little longer, but he had finished at the courthouse and he still had appointments waiting in his office. The quick introduction would suffice for the time being.

"I'd like to stay and visit, but I've got to get back to the office. I am expecting a client." The pain was excruciating knowing he had to leave her. Hank felt a stutter in his heartbeat; wishing everything and everyone else would disappear. He had left clients waiting before, but this one owed him money and that he needed.

"Okay. Well, thank you for helping me."

"My pleasure. Again, it was nice to finally meet you."

"You too."

She watched him scurry down the hall and make a

quick turn down the stairs. Jill found herself drawn to his beauty. She couldn't turn her eyes away until he had completely disappeared.

The lights of the Christmas display were gleaming in front of the courthouse. Santa's booth was quiet and dark. Jill wondered how many children had waited and wrestled the winter weather for a chance to give the jolly old man their Christmas wishes. She wondered too how many parents listened to make certain they would light up the hearts of their sons and daughters Christmas morning.

Working for the District Attorney's Office, Jill had become cynical about the role most parents played in their children's lives. It became all too familiar the destruction and despair that centered on the city youth. It felt like Jill had put the majority of Lubbock's parents in county jail or behind prison bars.

Christmas only three weeks away, Jill poured herself into her work. The only reminisces of the holiday in her apartment were a couple of festive cards sitting on the fictitious fireplace mantel. She had neglected to retrieve the Christmas tree from storage this year. No sense in decorating, it would be another holiday alone. Instead, she intended on renting old Doris Day and Sandra Dee movies and settling down to a warm turkey TV dinner.

Since the death of her father, many years ago, Jill has not been one for the holidays. She missed him everyday and when Christmas came around, it was just another reminder that he was gone. It was the one holiday that brought the entire family together, even if it were just for a few hours.

She recalled when her dad, a patrol sergeant, would finish the day shift and the family would be waiting impatiently, until he had shed off the heavy gun belt he had treaded around for eight hours. Jill remembered how excited she would become when she would hear the snap of his keepers and the Velcro of his vest. It meant he was only moments away from walking into the living room and handing out gifts, a wait she hated then, but something she missed now.

One Christmas in particular came to mind. She was eight or nine. Once her father had taken off the uniform and reclined in his worn out chair, she hurried to him with her gift. It was a porcelain figurine of a child with a street cop pulling a dirty teddy bear from a muddy pool of water, a proper homage to their relationship. Even at a young age, she knew the bond she and her father carried. Like the child in the sculpture, he was her hero. He meant the world to her and nothing could come between them and no one could make her feel as safe.

Wiping a couple tears from her cheek, continuing to push through the winter's wrath and the memory of her dad, she fumbled for her car keys. A gust of cold air brushed her face and like most days this December, she pulled her coat closer to her body. Dim gray clouds covered the sun, causing the air to feel as cold as a meat locker. With the packing plant northwest of town and a downward wind, it would be easy to convince visitors that they were standing in one.

Just then her cell phone rang and like all other

times, she fumbled to find it in her bag. Pulling it to her ear, she glanced at the flip phone's screen, it read, *unknown number*.

"Hello?"

"Hello?" asking again with attitude.

No answer. She put the phone back in her pocket and sat down in the car, started the ignition and at the same time turned on the heater.

The cold made the ten-minute drive feel like eternity. It was only as she pulled up to her apartment that the heat was beginning to thaw her toes.

Jared Shore, Lubbock's adorned District Attorney, allowed his staff to spend more time out than in. Jill didn't mind. She worked better with her compact discs playing and candles burning as she sat at her dining room table thumbing through case files and typing on her laptop. She had learned a long time ago that her home was her safe zone, serenity with no unexpected trespassers.

Some of the district offices were being re-carpeted and painted; remodeling that was badly needed and well over due. Jill's office was one of the few being modified. The small concrete dorm like room needed to be expanded, before a storage closet, now a promising attorney's fortress. Its solid walls and pale gray paint breathed dread and gloom, but Jill tried to give it character with photos and greenery. She didn't have much for art, but the office deserved more, so with a trip to the flea market and an occasional buy off the Internet, the office looked well decorated.

Jill arrived to her apartment just minutes after ten o'clock. As she walked up to her front door, with the cold air still encircling her body, she caught sight of her mailbox full of what looked like mail, which was strange, the postman usually did not deliver until after two o'clock in the afternoon. She assumed he wanted to finish his route before it got any colder.

After turning her key in the door and giving it a hard push, she sat down the bag she had been carrying and went back to pull the envelope out of the mailbox. Retrieving it, she placed the keys on a hook just behind the door, slipped off her favorite pair of Brighton flats and rested herself in an old worn out recliner.

Before sorting through the envelope, Jill noticed no return or delivery address; only '**Holland**' typed in a Gothic style font. Her curiosity and apprehension kicked in. Pulling out the first letter of seven, Jill became alarmed reading what was printed on the white piece of copy paper…

"*You are my soul mate, we belong together. We share the same friends, we share the same goals*".

Sorting through the letters, they all read about the same, except for the last letter…

"*I have watched you for too long. I want to come beside you, protecting you and caring for you. Don't worry about the past, your dad and Tucker they left you behind. You have let others die for you; I want to die with you.*"

CHAPTER TWO

IT DIDN'T TAKE LONG AND JILL HAD CONTACTED central dispatch, requesting someone from patrol to come and initiate an investigation and within minutes, an officer was at her door. Upon arrival, she gave the Lubbock Police Officer the letters, making a report of what she knew, which was not much. The only crimes committed were simple misdemeanors, but Jill felt safer creating a paper trail.

The short but stout Lubbock Police officer assured her that the apartment would be on close watch and would likely be contacted within the next couple days. Jill undoubtedly knew what that really meant. She would most likely be responsible to follow up with a detective and that her address would hang somewhere with many other "close patrols" and would be forgotten as the hour, day, night, and week went by.

Before the officer left, he dusted the mailbox for prints. Nothing seemed to surface. It could have been from the inexperience of the patrolman or the skillful planning of the person responsible, but either way, it was a useless effort.

The officer attempted to wipe away the orange florescent dust with a small portion of paper towel. It seemed the only good it did was spread the dust along the siding of her apartment and the snow lining the walk. Jill frustratingly told him to leave the residue; she would take care of the clean up. She thanked him and locked her door as he left.

Jill phoned Jared telling him that she would not be back to the office that afternoon. She explained the letters and wanted to stay near the house in case anything else came up.

Jared did not mind her absence; she was not due in court until after Christmas. He would be out as well. He and his wife were expecting their second child; his days were spent either in the doctor's office reading charts or in court reiterating testimony. He was beginning to think Jill might be better suited to run the office than he was.

In less than two years, Jill had acquired great status and successfully tried more cases than the any other attorney in Jared's office. The DA knew he had to take care of his most prominent assistant and told Jill how important she was and that he wanted to make her job there as easy as possible. She was the gem that made his staff shine, but she was never too arrogant to work any less.

Just as Jill hung up the phone, the receiver rang. It was Detective Rodgers from the Lubbock County Sheriff's Office. It had been some time since she had heard his voice, though they could go weeks without speaking and then spend an entire afternoon talking when some big case came up. This encounter, however, caught her off guard.

"Hello?"

"Jill? This is Rodgers. Hey kid, are you busy?"

"No, what do you need?" She was sincere but not too pleasant. She forced herself to see him as a cop and annoyingly fought the aspect that he was a friend. Even though Rodgers was there for her when her love life came to a grand finale more than five years ago, she just could not forget the miserable man Rodgers could be. She continued to only see his poor intentions and horny desires. Even when he was good, she knew better.

"I heard your place on the police radio and wanted to check and make sure you were okay. There was a reference to some letters left in your mailbox. What's that all about?"

Jill had no intentions with Rodgers, but he had every intention of winning her. When he first met Jill, all he did was lust after her, desiring nothing more than sex. Now, he only wanted to love her, but to convince her of that was easier said then done.

Mostly, Rodgers had been a sexist jock; looking down at women in a profession he thought was best fit for men, believing chicks only contribution to the job were hot numbers in tight uniforms and scapegoats when shit hit the fan. Yet recently, through Jill, he saw the benefits women provided the legal profession. He just hoped she never made him look stupid.

To the detective, their relationship had come such a long way. He could remember when Jill despised the idea of him being two feet away. Now she welcomed his calls, at least he thought she did. That alone was a big accomplishment for Rodgers.

"You know, the same old weirdo looking for a good laugh." Jill tried to hide her fear with laughter and joke, but the slight shake in her words caught the detective's ear.

Rodgers used to joke with her about her curtain of courage, how she would drape herself in it until the rain came and then the curtain couldn't keep her dry. He always reminded her that it was him that could feel the storms coming and that it was also him that held the towels that dried her off. She usually ignored his prideful banter and continued on believing she could take care of herself.

Jill told Rodgers what the letters read.

"It sounds a little more serious than some weirdo, who do you think sent them?"

Rodgers wished he could wrap his arms around her and let her know that she was safe. He wanted to protect her. Still enchanted by the attractive attorney, he fantasized about being with her, but he knew she was too smart for him and probably surrounded by lots of young, just as attractive, successful men.

"They weren't sent; someone walked up to my door and put them in my mailbox. There is no address or postage, just my last name."

Jill thought it was strange that only her last name was used. She had received letters at the office, but they were mailed and addressed to her as Jill Holland or Assistant DA. They were usually from disgruntled family members of defendants she pursued or the clients themselves once they had been sentenced. This batch seemed a little more personal.

The other end of the line went silent. Jill knew with the quiet, Rodgers was tapping his pen on the desk, scoping his office, and worrying about her safety. She had witnessed the same behavior before.

"I wouldn't get all concerned, I've seen worse." And she had.

Jill's life was not full of roses and chocolate. She had been through many hard times and drug through frightening ordeals. She could handle a few nasty letters.

"Look, if you need me, you know where to find me." He recognized her boundaries and decided to play defensively.

Jill thanked Rodgers for his trouble and with only a few more words, the two colleagues hung up the phone.

CHAPTER THREE

RODGERS LAID DOWN THE PHONE AND WANTED so bad to jump in his vehicle and drive to rescue Jill, but from what? She might be right, the letters might be part of a simple prank and there was no reasons to over react.

Rodgers had seen a special on the local news about Interest groups moving into Lubbock, prancing around government buildings with their signs and megaphones, preaching their agendas. He imagined Jill had prosecuted someone with a similar agenda and their following were angry enough to scare her, a bit Hollywood, but possible.

Even if that were the case, it was difficult for the detective to convince himself that she wasn't in danger. He had seen her go through so much over the last several years.

Despite their ability to tolerate each other, Rodgers and Jill's relationship wasn't always grand. He can still recall when Jill despised his entire existence. She would try everything and anything to keep from seeing him, routing her steps, planning her days, trying to keep from crossing the same path. It wasn't like that anymore. She had learned to overlook his flaws, not that she approved, she just accepted them.

Rodgers knew he was a cold man that many people avoided. Most were unable to digest his personality, others just didn't care. His character was hard and he had built a wall to keep people at a distance. It made doing his job easier, allowing him to concentrate on building cases and making arrest, but on the flip side, it made relationships harder.

Reserving only time for the badge, he lost touch with the things that made him happy, including his ex-wife. Her name was Jaclyn Michelle. She was his high school sweetheart and they married young, having three children before she reached the age of twenty-five. After twelve years of marriage, she saw Rodgers turn into a monster. He spent more time looking for criminals and less time with his family.

Jaclyn had told Rodgers repeatedly that he was changing. She was watching his kind personality mold into a cruel and cynical creature. She was not going to sit back while he persuaded his three boys to see the world as a volatile hole and women as a dense and lacking gender. Trying to do right for her children, Jaclyn moved back in with her mother and took the kids with her.

For years Rodgers blamed his ex-wife for ripping his children out of his life and cursed her for the divorce and everything else that came after. Jaclyn's words echoed in his head, day after day, year after year. She knew him better than anyone and pegged him as a chauvinistic, barbed, and ill-natured man. He didn't want to be that way, but after twenty years of the same behavior, it would take a miracle to change and a stronger miracle for Jaclyn to see the man he wanted to be.

Rodgers' temporary relief came from alcohol. Using the bottle, he attempted to escape his twister of reality. Plaguing his life with headaches and bad one night stands for more than three years, he slowly realized that the drink wasn't working and grew more suspicious, hated women more, and became a weekend dad.

The detective had the typical cop mentality, and struggled with the belief that women were the inferior sex and did not belong in a man's world. Thinking men were better, faster, stronger and smarter then any woman, he operated in an exemplary fashion of a chauvinistic man. His experience with ladies in uniform did not extend past the jail, limiting him to a small simple population of the American woman. The women in the locked facility acted like they were hard up and scared of a confrontation. His perception was that they were just shy of being real cops, either too dumb to take the test or too scared to fight alone. Wearing their uniforms a size too small and flirting with the inmates, even Rodgers thought they were a little too promiscuous. In reality, women were more than just jailers. Rodgers hadn't seen that until he met Jill.

Jill was feisty, determined, accomplished and professional, the perfect picture of the successful career woman. Doing what she was supposed to do, not caring who approved. Jill could think through an investigation before he could, she could shoot far better than he ever would and if truth were known, she could probably kick his ass. She was the package, the "I T" that he desperately feared in a woman.

The sheriff's office emerged from a small shell to the enormous entity it was now. Handing out more than two thousand paychecks, the Sheriff had quite an organization to run. He grouped his deputies according to experience, keeping balance; he made sure that there was always communication between agencies, his and all others.

The county dispatched for the sheriff deputies, Lubbock Police Department and occasionally for the Department of Public Safety. For the majority of the time, Texas DPS would go through their own dispatch, unless they were so far into the county their radios would not reach. Four years ago, the sheriff's department had gone to digital radios, including dispatch and The Highway Patrol were still using analog. That was the way the state was, low bid and less cost, even if it jeopardized its troopers.

Detective Rodgers made his way to dispatch to contact the officer that had responded to the call about the letters. Something had to be in the writings that would lead Rodgers to the culprit. Jill reading the words was not enough; he needed to see the threat.

The sight of the ladies sitting behind the microphones and small computer screens left Rodgers' desire for inner office romance short. It was like there had been a prerequisite set many years ago for the type of woman that worked the police radio. Their attitudes were as big as their waistlines. Rodgers attributed some of the weight to sitting in a dimly lit room for 10 hours a day and having only the high calorie snacks in the vending machine to keep hunger from striking. It didn't seem natural to have women of that size, with such disregard for human health to be the safety net that radioed the life to his officers. It amazed him how big some of the women would get. Regardless of his disgust for their figures, or lack there of, Rodgers needed to make contact with the Lubbock Police Department and the officer that had the letters and dispatch was his lifeline.

"Good morning Irene." Rodgers proudly stated as he walked in the door.

Irene was the lieutenant in dispatch. She had been there almost twenty years and had seen the sheriff's office become the monstrosity it was and grown with it. Irene was the biggest dispatcher on payroll. Rodgers was afraid of her, in fact most deputies were.

"Detective, what can I do for you this morning?"

"Who dispatched the officer to Assistant DA Jill Holland's residence this morning?"

"I was the one who sent the young man to her location. What a sweet girl she was, all-polite. Bless her heart; it must be hard being so pretty and single. I bet she has all kinds of freaks bothering her." Irene's concern was not genuine; she was more less fishing for gossip from the detective. Everyone was aware he knew Jill best.

Trying to stay on task, Rodgers asked, "Can you contact him and have him twenty-five with me at his department and tell him to bring the items collected from the scene." He walked away before she could ask any more questions. Shouting back from the door, he thanked her.

Rendering to the discretion of another agency was not easy for Rodgers. He was a proud cop that wanted to take charge in most investigations, especially those that involved people he cared about or in this case, loved. Despite the ability of the agencies to come together and assist each other or unite to run a search warrant, Rodgers would much rather work alone. Jill always told him that it would be his arrogance, not theirs, that would get him hurt.

Although he was not as fond of the Lubbock Police Department as Jill was, he brought himself to work along side of them when needed. Rodgers thought they were a smaller version of the Texas Department of Public Safety – Highway Patrol. He found the state trooper's style of policing to lack the community support that a law enforcement agency needed. He thought they acted like their training was the best, their manners were the greatest and that they could teach the sheriff's officer a thing or two. He found the Lubbock Police Department to act the same way.

Rodgers decided to meet with the Lubbock PD officer in the parking garage at the Lubbock Police Department. He wanted to see first hand the letters that were left to frighten his precious Jill.

Arriving to the parking garage, Rodgers could see the officer waiting at the far west corner. Hidden in a maze of slick Dodge Chargers, the officer was waving him towards his patrol car.

The detective recognized the officer from a fatal traffic accident investigation they had both responded to a month prior at the city limit line. It involved a retired police officer's granddaughter who had a lingering addiction. Apparently, the girl was a frequent customer for a local Methamphetamine dealer and after a quick smoke; she drove her car into a concrete wall. The trooper on scene had told them her skid measured more than 300 feet and after calculating the drag factor, her speed was estimated at 92 miles per hour. At that rate and force, there was not much left.

Rodgers and the Lubbock PD cop respectfully held the sheet that kept the media from filming the teen's exploded body. It was cold and sleet had fallen for more than an hour and in that time, the men hid the wreckage, never leaving the demolished life. Rodgers' remembered how his fingers grew numb and purple and that the officer had offered him gloves. He accepted and never forgot the charitable gesture; in fact he never returned the gloves.

The officer looked shorter then he did at the accident. He still had the calm demeanor and had developed a slight case of adult acne. His hair was longer; it had a feathery look, instead of the marine cut like before. He seemed to be carrying a little more weight, but it was of muscle, not fat. Rodgers had thought he was a brave and talented one and looking at him now, that hadn't changed.

Reaching out the envelope to the detective, the rookie stood back, giving Rodgers enough space to feel like he had privacy, but staying close enough to protect the evidence he needed to make his case.

"Staying busy?" The officer asked as he handed the detective a pair of latex gloves, hoping no prints would be destroyed.

"The county is full of nuts." Rodgers didn't have time for small talk and kept his answer short. "Thanks," he replied as he put on the gloves.

Reading each note and studying the severity of each threat, Rodgers was even more convinced this creep was serious. The words he read were words of warning. This was not just some prank. Jill was in trouble. Handing back the envelope and pulling off the gloves, he shook the officer's hand. The letters would stay with Lubbock PD, but the words would be etched in Rodgers' mind.

He sat back in the driver's seat of his unmarked unit and pulled a cigarette out from the crushed package of his shirt pocket. Too mad to light it, Rodgers let the cigarette hang from his lips, like a pelican gloating with its prize catch of the day. Focusing on each threat, gripping the stirring wheel, he began plotting his strategy in order to find the perp responsible for the new terror in Jill's life. This time he would be there to save her.

CHAPTER FOUR

J ILL MANAGED TO MAKE IT THROUGH THE WEEK with little worry. The letters had stopped and she had actually gotten some sleep. The work at the office had also provided some unexpected Christmas spirit. As she was preparing for court she got a phone call from the defense with an acceptance to an original plea offer.

She had a way of striking fear just before her moment in court that left the accused and their lawyer contemplating how much it was worth fighting for. Jill could convince a jury of a defendant's guilt before she was even through with the opening argument. There wasn't anything she did halfway. In court, it was no different.

Jill promised herself to take it easy over the weekend. A friend in her local Young Attorneys Club had prepared a bowl of pheasant dumplings as his contribution to the last meeting and sent a helping home with her. It was not her favorite dish, but she planned to devourer it for supper. After her meal, a warm bubble bath and a good book anticipated her company.

Closing the blinds of her small two-bedroom apartment she felt her phone vibrate against her thigh. Playing tug a war with a string that had gotten caught around the antenna, Jill finally managed to get the phone to her ear, not looking first to see who was calling.

Answering with a heavy voice, Jill uttered, "Hello?"

"Jill, this is Hank." Silence followed. "Hello?"

"Yeah, I'm sorry." Her admiration for him was

exposed in the giggle she gave at the end of her apology.

"I hope I'm not catching you at a bad time."

"No, I was just walking in the door from work."

"I was thinking about getting something to eat in town and thought you would like to join me?" He was so confident and forthright. His invitation jolted her and left her vulnerable, allowing only an answer of yes.

Forgiving herself for such weakness, she smiled. "Well, I had made plans with my couch and a few files, but I am sure I can reschedule." Which was not entirely true, but she knew for now she could get away with it.

"I will pick you up in about a half hour, does that sound okay?"

"Great, do you know where I live?" Jill was worried about the short notice, but was prepared to handle the rush.

Hank hesitated, as if he was not sure.

Jill continued, "You've seen the apartments on 19th Street and University?"

"The ones on the corner with the jacked up parking?"

Jill was all too aware of the parking situation at the complex. When the apartments were built, there was limited land and the spaces were painted perpendicular to the doors on each unit. She had perfected her parallel parking and invested in additional mirrors for her car.

"Yes, I'm in apartment twenty two, the corner one, with the small porch and a bench under the window. Just look for my white Lexis."

"Okay, I'll call if I have any trouble finding you."

She closed her flip phone and hurried to freshen up for her dinner date.

Jill could not believe how comfortable she was with this man she didn't even know. She was drawn to his masculine and smooth request. It was if she forgot her promise to ward off men and as if she condoned her fresh indiscriminate behavior.

It was obvious that Hank had quickly cast a strange magical power over her body and mind. She found herself aroused by his affection and attention. She might have easily fallen to his every wish. He could have asked her to change her political party loyalty and she would have. He could have asked her to jump off a ten-foot wall, in the nude, and she would have done that too. Hank was the man mother's warned their daughters about, the man father's feared their daughters would give their virginity to, the man right for someone, but giving himself to everyone. He was irresistibly dangerous.

No more than thirty minutes had passed and Hank was knocking on her front door. As she let him in, her appearance left him paralyzed in the middle of her kitchen floor. Standing with his ski cap in his hand, he was frozen with her appearance.

Jill had changed into a pair of dark denim Lucky jeans that exposed her luscious curves and tiny frame. She was draped in a pink cashmere sweater and adorned with pink beads, a gift from her brother in California. The blush colored pumps drew attention to dainty feet, complimenting the entire picture. She let her auburn hair fall against her back; clipping one side over, just above her eyebrows, exposing the exquisiteness of her green eyes.

Hank had not been out with anyone in an embarrassingly long time, since his fiancé, who remarkably resembled Jill, decided that marriage was not in her future. She wanted more than the West Texas way of life and surprised him with a 'Dear John Letter'. Hank was not as sad as most men might have expected him to be. He had grown tired of her high maintenance life style and looked forward to dating less pretentious women. It was therapeutic to find someone with such grace and yet still be modest and accepting of compliments, the way Jill seemed to be.

The admiration was returned. Jill thought Hank was a model of the perfect man. His personality and great features were too unique to ignore. Every time she saw him, she tussled with her craving to clutch her arms around his buff body. He stood nearly a foot taller and could swallow her up with his broad shoulders. Hank's muscles ripped through his shirt and etched out his fabulous build. His square jaw and inviting smile brought Jill to her knees. His dark curly hair rested on his neck and Jill tingled at the idea of running her fingers through it.

Waiting in her kitchen, Hank was wearing gap jeans with brown Doc Martins, a look that fit him well. The orange and brown striped shirt he wore that night, brought attention to his dark eyes and thick hair. Fastened no more than a few inches from his neckline was a gold chain. The color of his tanned skin perfected the way the jewelry laid. She wondered if even Hank had to pull himself away from the mirror once he dressed his well-kept body.

"Well, should we go?"

"Sounds like a plan." Jill picked up her purse; discretely decorated in pink and brown dots with a handle that was a softer shade of pink than the rest of the bag.

The winter weather had not given up. A chilly wind blew and Jill wrapped her arms around herself trying to keep warm. Her step got a little faster as they walked to Hank's truck. He opened her door and helped her inside. It was the kind of generosity Jill had imagined graced the streets of the old west, when cowboys helped their sweethearts into the wagons. She wasn't so impressed with his ride, though. It was an older model Chevy pick-up with bucket seats. The console was cracked and the stereo was missing. The floor mat was torn on her side and the one that should have been on the driver's side was gone. Jill didn't favor herself as being materialistic. Had she, the night would have been over then and there.

Turning on the heater, Hank asked, "How does Mexican sound?"

Jill was satisfied with the suggestion. She would have made the same choice had the decision been hers. "The warmer the meal, the better," Jill gave a shutter, clinching her teeth.

Pulling into the parking lot of the only truly authentic Mexican restaurant in town, she wondered if she would run into anyone she knew. What would the reaction be if they saw an assistant prosecutor having dinner with the County's public defender? Jill understood the ramifications, but more importantly and somewhat selfishly, understood the meaning of re-cues.

Over their chicken Quesadilla and cheese enchiladas, they discovered a lot more about each other than the matching profession and the pretty faces they flaunted. Hank was half American Indian, from a southern Cherokee tribe and half Irish. A unique combination, Jill would have like to have seen the oddity of that couple. His parents had divorced when he was nine years old and he had spent most of his life in Galveston, Texas, with the exception of the three years in law school. Hank had graduated from Baylor Law and spent a small amount of time with a D.C. law firm where he rubbed elbows with elite politicians and their under-minding team of lobbyist. Taking the name of his father's family, he returned to Texas as a public defender.

One of five kids, he was the only one to graduate from college, still believing there was hope for his younger siblings. He told Jill about their struggles back home and promised to help all he could.

"They're still young and have plenty of opportunities. I expect all of them to go on and finish school, at least undergraduate. My youngest sister is a thriving Liberal. She will be the typical college freshman, you know, the one who challenges everything and changes nothing." They both laughed thinking back to the days of college and simple life.

Hank continued to recall childhood memories and share with Jill the journey that brought him to Lubbock,

Texas. He told her that it was not his first time to the Raider city. He had lived there years back and visited often, knowing he wanted more.

"I dabbled in a political mess here in Lubbock and decided I wanted more of it." Not divulging too much, Hank announced that he recently got his own place.

"I had some issues with my last roommate. He didn't understand the concept of personal boundaries."

Jill understood that concept all too well. Rodgers was constantly testing its limits.

"My life has taken some major turns; it became inevitable that I needed to move out." Then with a little reluctance, he told Jill about his ex-fiancé, how he lost her to the charm of a big city horizon. "This town was just not big enough for both of us."

"I'm sorry."

"She said she needed to find herself," then with no warning, "what about you? Have you been lucky in love?"

She couldn't believe that he asked that question. She didn't expect to be rehashing her past and reliving the hurt on a first date.

Hank could see the surprise on her face and inquired, "Did I go too far?"

He didn't want to alarm her with his interrogation. "It's none of my business. I'm sorry."

It was common knowledge about Jill's days with Tucker and the murder triangle. It was the only thing people talked about for years and unfortunately, it labeled Jill. Hank too had known about it, but he was curious if there had been anyone else.

"I think everyone goes through trials and that

one day their *someday* comes." The phrase left the pair contemplating their future and considered the possibility of their new romance.

Jill changed the topic and saved the conversation by venting her qualms about her job and the uncertainties of staying in Texas. She was toying with the idea of moving to San Francisco and working with a Federal Prosecutor. She envisioned herself to be settled and married with children by the age of forty, although she wasn't about to tell him her time line, that she would keep a secret.

"My brother says I would love the West Coast. I just have so much history here, it seems unfitting to leave."

She finished with the story about her father's legacy. She spoke of the cowardly act of the youngster, now an adult, who sits in a state penitentiary for the shooting death of her dad, the best cop and man she ever knew.

"He did his job better then anyone. There was no way of avoiding his death, that teenager had his mind made up before my dad even went into the building."

Tears came to her eyes and before she broke into a familiar cry, she insisted that they leave so the restaurant could lock its doors.

On Friday nights the restaurant closed early. The bar attached, unlike the dinning area, was open until two in the morning, inviting the restaurant guest to an alcoholic beverage before parting ways. Jill had no intentions of visiting the bar or staying any longer.

She did however feel like a pampered lady that night. Jill had forgotten the last time a man picked up the ticket or even arrived at her doorstep to chauffeur her to a decent restaurant. What impressed her the most was that she could not stop talking and Hank could not stop listening. It was evident that they had a connection. A simple truth she was not willing to verbally admit, but a reality that neither was willing to ignore.

They returned to her apartment and an easy thank you was all that was spoken. Jill gave a slight wave to Hank, turned the key in the lock and paraded inside. Closing the door from the inside, Jill leaned against it, trying to wipe the smile from her face and trying hard not to lose her breath.

She felt the world trembling under her feet, fighting to keep on steady ground, knowing she was enormously attracted to him and could fall for him at any moment. She knew he was dangerous. The type of danger Superman found with Kryptonite or Batman had with Poison Ivy, worrying he would discover she was too feeble for his powers and would inevitably be pulled into his grips.

Hank was a professional bachelor, spending his time courting women with no real expectations. Jill knew the risks, but she envisioned she could win this battle. Like Hank, she too valued a challenge and she predicted a good one with the public defender, both in court and out.

Her cell phone began to vibrate from inside her bag, breaking the childlike crush behavior. The screen was lit with *Unknown Number*. When she answered and said hello she thought she heard someone sigh and then the line went dead.

"If it was important, they'll call back."

As she closed the phone, she remembered the letters. A little anxiety ran through her, but she forced herself to relax. The night was too good to be ruined by obnoxious pranksters. She would let the police know about the phone calls Monday morning; tonight she planned on enjoying the new itch she found in Hank and silenced her phone.

CHAPTER FIVE

MONDAY MORNING CAME TOO QUICKLY. THE sun was just as stubborn to get up as Jill was. After spending the majority of the weekend organizing photo albums and drawers, she was tired.

Jill had given herself the weekend off from her regular workouts and as a result, she felt the lazy temperament of her body. Classes at Tech were out for Winter break and the college kids had taken over her favorite gym. She decided to wait until after the holidays to get back in a routine, which inadvertently brought unpunctual mornings.

At six A.M. it was still dark outside and the apartment creaked with scary sounds. Jill could hear the neighbor's dog panting around her bedroom window looking for the precise place to leave his mark. The yellow snow around her back door said the dog preferred her porch to any other spot.

The complex shared the eastern side of the apartment. Although Jill's unit was considered separate from the other tenants, her back yard was connected to everyone else at the 19th Street Curryville Town Homes. From her back door, she had a visual on all her neighbors' living room windows. If they left the blinds pulled, Jill was witness to their everyday lives.

Her favorite neighbor was the elderly woman on the opposite corner. Jill would see the old woman leaving cat food out for the strays and dog biscuits for the dog that frequented Jill's back porch. She never spoke, but usually gave a warm wave, which was returned with a warm smile.

Jill suspected the old woman was all alone in life,

there were never any visitors and she remembered seeing the grounds keeper and maintenance personal checking in on her from time to time. Once, she had caught the elderly woman going through another neighbor's mailbox. Jill didn't point out the severity of the crime; she just pitted the old woman's loneliness.

As she dragged herself out of bed and in the direction of the bathroom, Jill wondered why Hank never called. Stepping into the shower, she remembered that she had silenced her cell phone Friday evening, after their date. If he had tried to phone, she wouldn't have heard it.

She was hoping he would try to catch her at the courthouse or in her office before the end of the workweek. If by then she didn't hear from him, it would be back to a professional relationship and no other small talk, unless approaching the bench.

Solitude had become Jill's preference. The less she spent with people, the less she was prone to get hurt. She enjoyed her quite nights and restful weekends, believing it was good for the soul.

Distance made the heart grow stronger; a cliché she lived by. It would be the same with Hank. She had no intentions of calling him. She would let him miss her first.

Getting dressed, she reflected on the tasks that she wanted to accomplish before noon. She would first call Lubbock PD and report the hang-ups that she had been getting. She thought there was a small chance they might be connected to the letters she found in her mailbox. It was also time to start preparing for another court appearance. Less then ten days before the holidays, she needed to contact people and file cases with the court. The judge was predictable about closing shop from the Monday before Christmas until the Monday after New Years Day. Jill knew a rush on the defense was always better for the State.

Adding to her responsibilities, Jill had to go by the Lubbock County Sheriff's Office to collect some statements the deputies had been so kind to gather. Creditable witnesses were hard to come by and Jill accepted all the help she could muster. The other assistants in the office had the idea that asking for help was beyond them, that an attorney had to build a case alone and with resilience. Jill looked at each case as a joint effort, between her and the department who filed the charge.

Finishing the last of the coffee, she ran out of excuses to avoid going to work. Grabbing her coat and brief case, she again hit the frigid air.

The morning traffic was fierce. The winter snow had fallen the night before and the snowplows and sand trucks delayed in getting the roads safe. It seemed the city employees slowed road preparation until there was an accident. Slipping and sliding, Jill managed to arrive to work later than expected, but safely.

Before going in, she had decided to contact the Lubbock Police Department, but all the day units were busy responding to wrecks and motorist assists. Mornings like this left little imagination to the workload of traffic officers and the Department of Transportation. Leaving no message with dispatch, she decided to call back later. Putting her phone down, she parked and went inside.

The halls were quieter than Jill predicted. The only one that had arrived before her was the office secretary, Beth. She was as diligent in her job as Jill was at her own. In fact, the two women secretly admired each other. Jill found it impossible to keep up with her order of business without Beth's organization and Beth found it impossible to be organized without Jill's style of productivity.

"Morning Beth, I see the weather couldn't keep you away. Are there any messages or rescheduled appointments?" Jill was sure someone had decided to make seeing her a least important priority.

"No one rescheduled, but it is still early. Someone did call for you, didn't leave a message. It was a man and he sounded irritated that you were not here." She rolled her eyes as she finished telling Jill about the call.

"He called restricted, so I do not have a call back number. I suggested transferring him to your voice mail, but he sounded like he was in a rush or something." Beth had an office to run and ironically had little patience for those with little patience.

Jill sympathized, "Well, if he needs my assistance he will have to get on the same page as this office. Next time he calls, just transfer him to my phone, whether I am in there or not. He can leave something on my voice mail. Thanks Beth."

Jill turned to make her way down the narrow hallway and enjoyed the unexpected quiet; she imagined that would soon change.

As she unloaded her bag on her desk, she

remembered she was supposed to have lunch with an old friend. She usually skipped the afternoon meal, but for Melissa Lynch, she would make an exception.

When Jill was preparing for the Bar Exam, she had met Melissa. Then just a single rambunctious law student, she had become an unimpeachable and respectable lawyer. The two began attending group study together and quickly built a trusting friendship. Both had similar dreams, but decided to practice law on two separate sides of the state. Melissa went to El Paso where she could practice immigration law and Jill stayed in Lubbock, where she felt most at home.

They had kept in touch with phone calls, emails and through Face Book entries. The last email Jill got was a reminder that Melissa was coming to town for her sister's wedding and that they should try to see each other. They planned to meet before Melissa's plane flew back south. Jill had missed her friend and her witty gossip. She could use a good laugh. It would be brief, but well cathartic.

"If I am going to get out of here by noon, I need to get things together." Jill thought to herself.

She started with a phone call to the sheriff's office to speak with the deputies and check if the witnesses' statements had been collected.

"Lubbock County Sheriff's Office," the voice was clear and firm.

"This is Jill Holland; I need to speak with Deputy," pausing for a moment and looking at her notes, "Tyler, L504."

"He is on a call right now, can I take a message?"

"Could you let him know that I will be by to pick up

some statements he had obtained for me? He can leave them with Detective Rodgers if he won't be available."

"Who is this again?"

"Assistant DA, Jill Holland."

The woman said that she would notify him by radio. Jill thanked her and hung up the phone.

It didn't take long for her to wrap up the morning details and decide to get out for some fresh air. She left everyone at the office around eleven o'clock and drove over to the Lubbock County Sheriff's Department. The weather had cleared and the sun was shinning, yet still cold, she clung to her coat.

It was amazing how far the building had come. For more than five years, the County too had been remodeling. The Sheriff's Department had gone from an abandoned shell to a polished and rejuvenated historical office space. The inmates were still housed at the original jail, but the offices were moved to the redesigned building.

Jill made her way to Detective Rodgers' office.

"Hey kid," Rodgers was quick to say when he saw her move through his door. It was like she had wings. Her body glided across the floor.

"Hello, do you have a minute?" Jill could see a stack of folders on his desk.

"Yes, always. What can I do for you?" His tone was a little condescending, but Jill ignored that. His eyes scanned her body and Jill tried to ignore that too.

"I'm here to pick up some witness statements for a

case. The deputy who had taken the initial call had said he would get the statements for me. I told him to leave them with you if he wasn't going to be available." She referred to him by his badge number, L504. Jill never could recall the deputies' full names; it was by luck that she could even remember their badge numbers.

"Right, he told me you would be coming by. Tyler said he would probably be in the patrol room, dictating a report. The statements are in his locker. You will have to give him a minute until he finishes recording. I'll call the secretary and let her know you are headed that way."

Shifting the topic, Rodgers was hoping she would join him for a casual bite.

"Do you have plans for lunch?"

"Actually, I am meeting an old friend, but maybe I can catch you some other time?"

"Sure." His sorrow for the rejection was quickly smothered with jealousy for the sap that was taking her to lunch. Though Rodgers was disappointed, he was too proud to let it show.

With a shake of hands and a quick direction of where she could find the deputy, the two said good-bye.

CHAPTER SIX

J ILL QUICKLY HEADED FOR THE DEPOT DISTRICT. It was a popular social place in Lubbock. Weekends, the bars and restaurants would be crowded with Tech students raging with wild hormones. The streets jammed by vehicles and college youth with a new sense of freedom. During the week however, the district was more for the professionals who needed a place to kick back with less crowded roads and a quite background.

Jill was looking forward to seeing Melissa. The last letter had included a picture of her and her new fiancé. She recalled how happy the couple looked; giving the impression that marriage life was a bond of true happiness. Jill envied her newly engaged friend for only a minute. The man, the ring, even the dress all came with baggage. As much as she wanted companionship, she also wanted her independence.

At the edge of the Depot District was a small family diner the two girls frequented during their short time together. Never really crowded, the girls loved the atmosphere and the ice tea was sweetened to perfection. It seemed fitting that they meet there for old times.

Jill recognized Melissa the moment she walked in the doors. Her smile was so charming. Her black hair was pulled up in a clip with a few loose strands of hair scooped behind her ears. Wearing a light blue swag skirt with a thin long sleeve blouse and open toe pumps, Melissa seemed dressed for the beach. Regardless what the temperature registered outside, she forever dressed light. Her mere presence was enough to make it feel like summer. The glow from her body made people feel warm and cozy, like they were standing on hot sand, cuddled with joy as if they wrestled it between their toes.

Melissa stood taller than Jill, about six inches. She was long and thin, but not too thin. Her legs looked like they extended to her neck; the few curves left little to the imagination. Jill remembered how much attention Melissa would get during college, not only from men, but from women as well. She was an attractive woman and easy to fall for.

"Jill!"

"Melissa, how are you?" Jill asked as she made her way between the hard wooden table and chairs and embraced her friend.

"Great, how have you been?" Melissa wrapped her arms around Jill's petit frame and kissed her slightly on the cheek. They held hands for a moment before sitting down.

"I am so glad you called. How was your sister's wedding?"

As the two women reminisced, the waitress arrived with water and menus.

"Beautiful!" Taking a sip from her water, she added, "too much money though, Ceremonies are overrated." Pulling pictures from an envelope, she added, "Phillip and I plan to elope."

Jill envied Melissa's rambunctious lifestyle and vicariously lived through her stories. She wondered if marriage was going to slow her friend down or speed things up.

"I wish my visit wasn't so short. I'm disappointed I can't spend a little more time with you and maybe see some of the old crew from Tech. Which reminds me, you will never guess who I ran into?"

Jill looked up from her menu with a puzzling stare.

Placing her hand on Jill's shoulder, Melissa answered, "Troy Scott."

Both girls began to laugh. Troy Scott was a sophomore at Texas Tech University when Jill was finishing her law degree. He was a skeletal looking freckle face boy, majoring in communications, following Jill everywhere, and pointing a camera in her direction when at all possible.

Troy had met Jill one afternoon at the University library. Troy was twenty and Jill had him convinced she was only approaching thirty, but still too old for him. Jill thought it was flattering, but was glad when the admiration eventually disappeared.

"Do I even want to know what he is doing?" Jill was beginning to blush. Stirring the lemon in her water, she had made her selection off the menu and waited to hear about her old admirer.

"He told me he was working for a local news broadcasting station as a production assistant. I didn't talk long. I was at the Wal-Mart on 34th and Milwaukee buying stockings for the big day and he was holding a hairbrush. I'm not sure why, he has very little hair left."

The woman laughed again. Melissa went on to tell her that he was fit, bigger, "looked like he has been working out. You should give him a call; he was exceedingly cute."

Jill just rolled her eyes at her sassy friend.

"Really Jill what are you going to do, stay single for

the rest of your life? Not everyone is so terrible." She knew Jill was shy at getting involved again.

No one knew just how much Jill feared being hurt. Life hadn't been sympathetic when it came to her heart. Men just weren't what she needed or wanted now in her life. She liked being her own best friend. Besides, she felt safest alone.

Giving the waitress their orders, Jill responded, "I know. I just can't seem to find my prince charming."

Melissa sensed the sarcasm in Jill's voice. "No one finds their prince charming sitting in a run down diner with their girlfriend and if they do, it is too late.

Over salads, the two sifted through the photos from Melissa's sister's wedding. Photo after photo, the girls pointed to a few people they recognized from college. Everyone looked happy; it seemed the day was a proud one.

"Your sister looks so happy."

"Jill what are you waiting for? Are you even looking?" Melissa didn't want to see her friend old and alone. Life was short she wanted Jill happy too.

"If I were looking," Jill answered with a wink. "He would have to be someone who knows what I want. A man who doesn't need me to tell him, a man who feels it in my heart beat." She paused and then, "I don't want to ever be second best. You know, find out two years into the marriage that your spouse made the sacrifice, and wishing they had waited for something better, or worst, finding him with that something better."

As Jill spoke, Melissa was captivated and listened to her poetic script of her fairy tail wish. At the same time she could feel the burden of her friend's pain.

"My wish is to find that one person you go to bed dreaming about and then wake up lying with."

Jill thought about the idea of someone holding her at night. She wanted to be loved, but the repercussions that came with that were too great to risk. Her depiction of what she needed would keep her friend from intruding any further into private life.

The two women finished their lunch and promised to keep in touch. Leaving the restaurant, Jill asked Melissa how she could go anywhere without a coat.

"I'm not a baby!" Like a scene in a movie, Melissa swung her hand in the air, twirled around with the sun casting an extraordinary outline of her sleek silhouette.

Before Jill could say anything more, Melissa was in her car and Jill's cell phone was ringing. Waving bye, Jill pulled it from her coat pocket and said "hello?"

Again, "Hello?"

Jill couldn't get anyone to answer, and then just before she hung up…

"Did you enjoy your lunch?" It was a husky voice. The man's voice was familiar, but Jill could not place where she had heard it before.

"Nice to catch up with old friends, isn't it?"

"Who is this?" Jill's voice trembled as she spoke. She was debilitated with scared emotion.

"Your admirer. It's great to see you laughing again."

The line went dead. Looking around the parking lot, she saw no one. Without hesitation, Jill called Detective Rodgers.

CHAPTER SEVEN

"SHIT!' RODGERS WAS OUT OF AMMO AND HE had two more shots to make, it would cost him valuable points at final count. Regretfully, he cleared his weapon and stepped aside for the Chief Deputy to score his targets.

Rodgers was a bit eccentric when it came to weapon qualifications. He was known for practicing numerous times before the actual event and cleaning his weapons even more for optimal performance. Dressed in his dark cargo pants with several pockets, all packed full of empty magazines. His duty weapon, a .357 Glock, bundled on his hip and attached to his thigh was his off duty Kel Tec 9 mm. Adorned with an extra magazine holder, his AR-15 laid still on the table behind him. Rifle qualifications were always first and most everyone could shoot the beast with much accuracy.

Rodgers prided himself in the ability to score in the top ten percent. The younger deputies watched the detective, looking for helpful hints to better their own game. Rodgers always said, "You have to show up long before the battle begins. Preparing on the front line was only preparing for defeat."

The state required 70%, and he usually ended up with a score between 93 and 94 percent. This time would be different. Rodgers heard the Chief Deputy who was also the range master, shout out his score. "89"!

It was expected. He couldn't get Jill off his mind and it was affecting his game. You don't come to the range and be distracted or finish without enough rounds and expect to score your best. Rodgers knew he would be on the range this weekend, shooting until his score was better.

The sun was out that afternoon. The 30-degree morning temperature was rising and it was beginning to feel more like 50 degrees. Rodgers had worn three shirts and it had heated up down range. As he was taking the top shirt off, labeled with large white blocked letters that read SHERIFF, he felt his phone vibrating on the inside of his bulletproof vest.

Phones were not allowed on the range because of the obvious dangers. But, Rodgers superciliously disregarded the rule and had made a make shift pocket on the inside of his body armor for occasions when he needed his phone more than he needed compliance.

He walked to the men's out door toilet stall and closed the door. The odor and the thick walls kept out ranking officers and protected him from ramifications for his flagrant disregard for policy. Reaching inside his shirts from the neckline, Rodgers fumbled to retrieve his phone. It was thin and weightless, which made carrying it convenient, but retrieving it, a hassle.

Once he managed to get the phone out, the vibration stopped. Touching the picture end he could see who called. It was Jill. He quickly began to dial her number, but before he could finish, the phone began to vibrate again.

"Hello? Jill, are you okay?"

"Rodgers, I am at the Cannon Family Diner. I just got the strangest phone call on my personal cell. I think this freak is watching me." Jill's words were shaky.

"Is anyone around you?"

"No, I am in my car in the south parking lot."

"Lock your doors, I am on my way. I am at the gun range. Let me check in my rifle and I'll be there in ten."

Rodgers flew open the bathroom stall door, not caring who saw him with a phone. His only concern was to get to Jill and to find this perp.

Jill was sitting in her vehicle when Rodgers arrived. She had forgotten that the Lubbock County Sheriff's Office had their bi-annual shooting qualifications that afternoon until Rodgers stepped out of his unit wearing what Jill would consider the typical raid uniform. Cargo pants tucked in Danner duty boots and several cop tools dangling from his waist. Not to mention the two guns attached to his body, passively tempting evil.

With a sense of relief, watching Rodgers bravely march to her vehicle, she unlocked her doors and got out of the car.

The frantic picture brought Rodgers to do something he had never done before. Walking, almost running, he wrapped his arms around Jill and asked, "Are you alright?"

Returning his hug, Jill nodded yes into his shoulder.

"Where is your phone?" Rodgers was looking at her hands, watching impatiently for her to release it from her grips.

Handing it to him, Rodgers waited no time to scroll down through the received calls and by no surprise; the call had come in private.

"I'll submit a fax to the cellular company. Who is your service with?"

"Sprint."

"They might be able to give me a number or at the least a location of the tower used."

Jill knew it was nearly impossible to trace the line. She had tired numerous times with her cases and had gotten nowhere. This person was watching her and there was nothing she could do about it.

"Is this the only time he has contacted you?"

"I have gotten a few hang-ups, but I couldn't be sure they were related."

"Alright," Rodgers' eyes and voice mirrored anger, "now he has crossed the line. This prick has made it personal. I will follow you to your apartment. I want you to gather some clothes. You are staying with me." He spoke with domination. He gave no room for debate. Jill needed to be in his protection until they figured out how serious and desperate this man on the other end of the phone could be.

She whispered, "Okay". Moving slower than before, she wished now she had someone to hold her tight.

CHAPTER EIGHT

TROY SCOTT WAS A MAN OF DISTINGUISHED morality. He had spent the majority of his adult life volunteering at homeless shelters and donating what extra money he had to crisis centers. Since graduation from college, all his free time was spent entertaining broken hearted women and their troubled children. Most nights, he would serve hot meals to disadvantaged families, wash bed linens from the uncomfortable cots they slept on, or play card games with misguided adolescents. As if that wasn't enough, he spent extra time with women who didn't want to be alone and chaperoned kids to museums and parks as often as possible. He even found himself falling for some of the children, which wasn't against policy and not that unethical.

Before Troy came to know the families at the shelters he had acquired a co-op job as a camera operator for KVVI Channel 20, a major news station in Lubbock, Texas. After relentless begging, Troy found himself interning with the best at the news station. As a sophomore in college, he buried himself in every opportunity the station allowed. There were stories about wild dogs and even more boring stories about baking the best country brownies, but then there was one story that changed everything; 'Murderous Plot results in death of local Pharmacist'. He couldn't remember all the details, but became fascinated by the circumstances and captivated by the people involved. It was the one story that made the others worth filming. The story of the love affair between Tucker Stiles and the criminal investigator, Jill Holland, sparked news when she defended herself at the firing of a single bullet.

Troy eventually used the story as inspiration with the woman at the shelters, ensuring each one of them that they too could be so strong. He retold the strength that Jill had held on to and that she had become better than the man that mistreated her. He found himself thinking about this stranger everyday and dreaming about her almost every night.

After the reported scandal, Troy was sorting through old newspaper articles from the slide archives in the grand library; Jill had approached him and asked for help with the machine she was using. He quickly recognized her from the piece.

"Excuse me, I'm having trouble getting the screen to scroll down, is there some kind of trick to this?"

She did not notice Troy's eager expression as he got up from his chair to assist.

"This machine acts up all the time. If you get here before noon, you have a good chance of getting one of the good ones." Troy banged on the machine a few times, until the librarian cleared her throat as if to tell him to stop. He remembered them both chuckling.

"Thanks. I'm Jill."

"Troy." He sat back down and nothing more was said.

Troy tried everyday to see her, arranging a casual encounter on campus. It might be at the soda machine near the library or the ATM at the Student Union Building. Sometimes he would witness her enjoying life around Lubbock, but that was rare. He subconsciously memorized her schedule, looking for every opportunity to have a conversation with her and eventually, to his surprise, found the courage to ask her out.

One morning Jill was sitting on a bench outside the Fine Arts Building on the West side of campus, one of the many places to soak up the extraordinary scenery on Tech's campus. The tall structures surrounding the spot, disguised the city that sat on the borders of the college, giving the allure that the school was free of filth.

Summer semester was in session for the undergraduates and the law students were preparing for the Bar Exam, including Jill.

"Good morning Jill."

She turned to him a little startled and followed his greeting with an effortless hello.

"Studying for the Bar?" He sighed, recognizing the ignorance of his question and felt the powering nervousness that caused him to ramble.

"Yes, Troy. Did you need something?" She glimpsed up from her notes, only to see where he was standing.

That was the first time Troy felt insensitive words from her and the first time he considered being angry.

"I have tickets to a live production of 'Texas', would you like to come with me? It is performed in the scenic canyons of Palo Duro State Park. The drive is less then two hours and it will give us time to get to know each other."

"The gesture is sweet, but I'm busy." She patted his arm with a light tap, gathered her books and said goodbye.

He wondered if her refusal was actually a carried fear from her strain with Tucker or the brutal reality that she was not interested. It didn't stop him though. He would ask many times more and she would always say no and then point out the young hotties on campus, hoping to ease the rejection.

"They would love to go out with you." She would wink and walk away.

As time passed, Troy finally let go of the dream of being with Jill. She had gone on to bigger and better things. He remembered the man she chose and saw the life she wanted, those two things he could never be. Maybe one day the two could be together, but he knew it would have to wait. He would stay hidden, but close enough incase she needed him.

Aspiring to be the camera production manger, he had to bury himself in boring stories, work extra hours and follow whatever leads the news anchor suggested. The first of many feed his compassionate side and eventually helped to promote him and which lead to his relationships at the shelters.

Lubbock was loaded down and crowded with abused women and their children, unfortunately most Texas cities were. The problem was growing so fast, programs and laws could not keep up and women were flocking to shelters or dying. Troy became aware of the problem while doing the story on government handouts and 'who was really paying the cost'. The news anchor suggested they air from a woman's shelter and create public awareness and more emotional effect. Troy opened his eyes to the apathetic approach by society to fix these families. He had seen more lives destroyed by the ignorance of Texas' fathers then by freak accidents or major violent crimes. He was frustrated by the government's lack of commitment to protect the women and even more frustrated at the men who were responsible for their afflictions.

He cloned the concept and term "redneck mentality". Troy alleged that the more intense the abuse, the lower the level of education the abusers held. He believed education was the tool needed to set everyone free. Many hours were spent researching and lobbying for more grants to fund classes for the women in the shelters and education for the dads. Troy found himself going back to the shelter again and again, making it a necessity. He cast himself as a martyr, not for the purposes of looking like a hero, but because he really cared. The people at the shelter became his family and Jill's memory became his fantasy. He looked forward to the evenings and weekends with his "trusted goof troop", even if it was behind the thick walls of the shelters.

The battered women and children were among some of the people who appreciated his efforts. The City of Lubbock awarded Troy Citizen of the Year, two years in a row. The City recognized him for his unselfish deeds and for his ability to console the families and assure them about their uncertain future, a bright light to their dark days. It was an honor, inspiring him to return night after night, month after month.

Troy's caring side was not his only side and to be captured as a gentle man was a great accomplishment. Developing as a child from the witnessing account of his mother brutally raped and beaten, he had spent years struggling to overcome anger and violent tendencies himself. Troy remembered at the young age of twelve, hiding under his bed, listening to his mother's screams, scared the man would come for him next.

The man, who was also his neighbor and friend, had presented himself as individual with good intentions. His veneer of a considerate person, fallaciously wanting to help a single mother who was left to raise her small child alone, created a lying friendship. Dropping in from time to time, hand delivering groceries, tending to yard work or assisting in garbage removal, Troy's mother felt obligated to invite him over for dinner; it was an invite that changed their family forever.

The nightmare crafted a bond between Troy and his mother, stronger than any average mother and son. They were best friends and relied on each other for everything and trusted no one about anything. Troy lived with her until he was twenty-two, throughout college and a short time during his career at KVVI news station.

He didn't know it, but his mother was suffering from terminal cancer and had only months left. Realizing that she would be leaving Troy alone in the world, she needed to make him strong and independent from her. With nothing more than a note, she told him it was time to move out, leaving him alone and scared. Swallowing his tears and convinced he was supposed to fight for everything in life; he accepted his fate and moved on.

Troy quickly found an apartment near the news station. More than 1400 sq. feet, it provided enough space for a roommate, someone who could help share the bills and hide the silence. No more than a month had past and Troy was showing the place to several perspectives. With no one appealing to his personality, he called the first guy on the list and told him the room was his. In just six weeks, Troy had a new home with a new roommate and a new perspective on life.

Everything was looking up, summer had come and gone and winter had made a modest entrance. Since his move, Troy had received a promotion and a substantial raise. He also discovered the roommate he had chosen for the empty room had a poor personality and unhealthy qualities he couldn't ignore. With little regret, he told him to leave.

His life was falling into place, until a Saturday afternoon in mid November. Sitting on the front porch, enjoying the unusual winter weather, a patrol car drove up along the curb. Two young peace officers got out and walked toward him.

"Sir, are you Troy Scott?" One asked as he pulled off his hat and adjusted his portable radio volume.

"Yes sir." Troy imagined that it had something to do with his disgruntled roommate. Troy was not prepared for the news that came next.

"I'm afraid I have some bad news. Your mother has died."

Troy looked down at his hands, folded on his lap.

"Are you alright sir?"

Troy didn't speak, only nodded his head.

"Is there someone I can call to be with you?" The officer was sincere and knew it was never a good idea to leave the mourning alone.

"I would like to be by myself."

Troy had no one. His mother was the only one left in his life and he had just thrown out his roommate.

College was over and he didn't really know his co-workers.

"Sir, is there is someone I could call?" The officer asked.

Troy looked at the officer again, giving this time a look of affirmation for them to leave.

The officers gave the grieving son the numbers for the hospital and the funeral home where she had been taken. They returned to the patrol unit and drove away.

Troy picked himself up from the porch step, dusted off his pants and went inside to drink a beer.

CHAPTER NINE

THEY NEVER LOST SIGHT OF ONE ANOTHER. In unison, giving the impression they were attached at the grill, the cars parked in front of Jill's apartment. Jill and Rodgers got out in the same fashion.

Walking in, Rodgers noticed the way Jill kept house, clean and uncluttered. He was impressed with her style, reminding him how much of a bachelor he had become. Decorating the kitchen in country roosters, the touch was soft, but hard enough to grab his attention.

Making their way to the dinning area, he made a joke about the cocks in the kitchen, a room oriented for females. Jill shoved him to the side and gave a short frown for the joke told at such a fragile moment. Even then Rodgers couldn't help being himself.

Glancing around the room, Rodgers noticed no Christmas decorations, thinking it was unfit to be alone for the holidays.

"How long do I need to pack for?" Jill hollowed from the bedroom.

"At least through the week, I will get Lubbock PD on it as soon as I get back to the office. You on the other hand need to work from my place. The DA will just have to live without you."

Evaluating the situation she was in, Jill made no argument. She was beginning to understand how dangerous the mystery man might be.

She quickly gathered her things and followed Rodgers out to the cars.

He suggested she leave her car at the sheriff's office. "No one will bother it there, squad cars will do close patrol until I tell them otherwise. I don't want this creep knowing where you are and what you are doing."

"Thank you Rodgers." Jill was scared and it was Rodgers who reassured her again that things would be all right.

Five years ago, Jill was challenged by greed and power. She had to fight for her life, not only to survive, but also to hold on to the strengths that made her a strong woman. It was Rodgers who had saved her from that evil named Tucker Stiles. Now, like then, it was Rodgers who came to her rescue.

After parking her car at the sheriff's office, Jill went to Rodgers. As she put her two bags in the back seat, Jill reflected on the fact that someone wanted to scare her and it was working. Her bulky brief case in her lap, with the seat belt annoying her neck, she anticipated an awkward week with the man she slightly adored for holding her up when times got rough.

The ride to Rodgers' home was like other rides with him. The window was cracked just enough to suck out his cigarette smoke yet still chocking Jill with the smell. She hated the fact he could fill his lungs with such a nasty craze. She despised the tobacco companies and the ads they endorsed ever since she lost her grandfather to emphysema. She remembered as a teen, watching such a God-fearing man and lively creature dwindle into nothing, murdered by the curse of nicotine. Now she wondered how long it would be until she would see Rodgers fall to similar fate.

Strangely the wind was no more. West Texas

glorified itself in the ability to blow air 365 days a year. When the rareness of no breeze presented itself, people took notice. Jill had. Of course, she was noticing everything that seemed unusual.

Pulling into the drive, Jill noticed nothing about Rodgers' home looked the same. His lawn was brown from the winter weather. No evidence of dead flowers or even weeds to say summer had once been there. The swing that was so inviting some time ago was still latched to the front porch, but now was faded and the chains were rusted. Jill thought it would probably fall from the hooks if anyone dared to take one swing.

Approaching the door, Jill's phone rang. Looking with anticipation and grief, she read the caller ID. With a slight smile and sigh, she told Rodgers it was okay.

"Hello?" Even after such an afternoon, she was ecstatic to finally get a call from Mr. O'Donnell.

"Hello Jill. Are you busy?" Not waiting for an answer he continued, "I was calling to apologize for taking so long to get back with you. Things have been hectic. I wanted to tell you that I had a wonderful time on our date and wondered if you would like to join me again tonight for drinks?" Hank had hoped that he could convince her it was worth it and get to spend some more quality time with his new passion.

"Well, um, I guess a drink wouldn't hurt."

Only one foot in the doorway, Jill could smell the residue of bachelorhood.

"Great. How about 6 o'clock, I'll pick you up?"

"Actually, I will meet you. Where do you want to go?"

Hank did not need to know that she was staying with Rodgers. She didn't want to explain anything.

"Let's try the Fifth Season Hotel Bar. I hear it has a great atmosphere."

"Great, I'll see you there."

Laying her phone down, Jill could sense a little tension from Rodgers. He walked around the kitchen without speaking. Before she could escape to another room, he retrieved a glass from the freezer and invited her to some wine. Hesitantly, Jill sat down at his dilapidated kitchen table, watching him pour the White Zinfandel into a lightly frosted glass. Sipping the wine, she noticed he wasn't having any.

"Aren't you going to have a glass?"

"I got to get back to the range." Rodgers had to clean his weapons. "I will lay out some clean linen and towels. You can stay in the blue room across the hall from mine. I don't guess I need to baby sit you, it sounds like you have enough men watching over you." Rodgers' tone was accented with jealously.

Jill was not in the mood for his candor.

"If you think by inviting me to your home is an opportunity for you to rain your egotistical and narrow male reasoning over me, you better back up mister." Jill stood up from her chair and turned to leave the room. Forgetting her phone on the table, she turned back around and waited for some kind of response.

He said nothing.

She walked through the hall and into the bedroom and began emptying her bag. It wasn't long before Rodgers came to the doorway.

"How do you plan to meet your friend? Your car is

at the station." Rodgers took delight in proving anyone wrong, especially if it meant he was right.

Sitting on the edge of the bed and huffing loud enough for him to hear, Jill asked, "Can you take me to my car?"

She was beginning to think the arrangement had been a bad idea. Rodgers had started his impeccable self-righteous attitude and she wasn't sure she could tolerate one night. She needed a drink and looked forward to seeing Hank again.

"Fine." It was still early, but Rodgers told her he would be ready in five minutes and he wasn't going to wait for her to primp and powder.

He watched her sitting in his car, looking beautifully annoyed. Rodgers couldn't help but smile, she too return the grin thinking to herself how ferociously predictable he could be. Opening the driver's side door, Rodgers sat down.

From the passenger seat, Jill slugged his arm. "You drive me crazy. Take me to my car."

As if she could see that he was genuinely concerned, she added, "I won't be long. I'll call when we finish our visit." Reaching for his hand as Rodgers shifted gear, she said, "I'm thankful for everything you do and for being there when I needed you." Their eyes met and as quickly as they met, Jill looked away.

In a split second Rodgers felt the difference between affection, lust and love. He took a deep breath. Jill was more than his friend. The fact was he loved her and he wasn't going to let her get away this time.

CHAPTER TEN

ANK WAS ALREADY WAITING FOR HER WHEN she arrived. He hadn't been there long, no drink was on the table and he was still wearing a coat. Under his jacket was a white suit shirt tucked neatly in faded blue jeans, accented with a wide brown belt and what looked like brown Harley boots. The look was casual, but classy. Jill remembered how his striking good looks took her breath away when he collided with her in the courthouse. As he stood from the table, the air escaped her again.

The Fifth Season Bar was busier than Jill expected. People lined the walls and only a few tables were left empty. Darkly lit and reeking of stale beer, the bar gave an air of obscurity, inviting the inhibited and giving hope to the lonely. Despite the sinful atmosphere, Jill felt pathetically comfortable.

The two sat down near the entrance, with their backs to the wall. Jill always liked to keep an eye on who came and went, whether she was at home, the office or some place public, it didn't matter where; she didn't like being on the receiving end of surprise.

Hank motioned for a waitress and took the liberty of ordering two Cape Cods with extra lime. Jill looked at the waitress and agreed with slight irritation in her voice. Granted, she loved Cape Cods, but couldn't recall telling Hank.

"How have you been?" Hank asked.

"Busy. Fixing what defense attorneys crush can exhaust an entire prosecuting team." She smiled at the jab towards Hank. He smiled back accepting her humor. "How have you been?"

"The same, defending mostly juveniles and irritating Prosecutors," Hank shifted his body towards hers, nudging her elbow and smiling with his returned jab. "But seriously, I feel like I am the only trusted adult they have." Hank's office defended more juveniles' then adult criminals, a nuisance that followed most public defenders.

"I'm assigned to one boy who lost his mother at the age of 15 to a drug overdose, leaving him to raise his younger sister. She has a disorder that causes her eyesight to deteriorate; only adding to the boy's mounting problems." Hank's eyes scurried the bar as he spoke. He was impatiently looking for the waitress.

"Three weeks ago, the same boy was arrested for stealing a vehicle, trying to get his sister to an optometrist. The doctor agreed to treat the girl free of charge, but his office is in Abilene. Get this; the car the boy stole was his dad's, the man that deserted him when he was only 9 years old."

Jill shook her head in disbelief. She could feel the pain in Hank's voice.

"Well, the dad pressed charges and now, at the age of 17, he is facing lock up." Hank nervously rolled the paper napkin that awaited his drink.

"The dad makes me so irate. Those are his flesh and blood. What do those kids have to do to make him love them?" His voice was getting louder.

Just then the waitress sat down their drinks. Hank tipped the young woman and asked her to start a tab.

The waitress kindly averted, but her tired sad eyes stayed with Jill. Dressed in a University of Texas tank and a small denim skirt, wearing a tender smile that was flattered by her long soft-blond hair, masking her true identity behind the muffling bar smoke and dirty men, Jill guessed the girl was no more than twenty years old.

Jill wondered if the waitress was working for her education or if the girl had been lost to the way of the college town, fighting physically and financially to survive. She questioned if the waitress had been forgotten in the mess of the world, or beaten down so hard, that she was stuck waiting on men who saw her only as a piece, not as a prize?

Diverting back to Hank, Jill asked, "Why hadn't the State placed the children in a foster home?"

"The paternal grandmother, who is no better than the biological father, agreed to have the children stay with her. Unfortunately, the boy ended up taking care of all of them."

Drinking from her glass, Jill made a mental note to add lime next time she made a Cape Cod. Hank's recipe was much better than her own.

"I think it is great how you taken an initiative to help so many people, Hank."

"Jill you do that too. Most attorneys in you office, hell in most offices, can't keep up with your compassion for your work. You look out for the people in this county, I think that is great. I limit my skill to one person per case. So who really is the helpful one?"

Flattered by his remarks, Jill held up her glass for a toast and Hank ordered another round.

Continuing to make small talk, time seemed to slip

away. Before she knew it, several hours passed and several drinks had been consumed. Shortly after ten o'clock, Jill decided it was time to say goodnight and return to Rodgers. Only, when she stood to go, she stumbled, catching herself in Hank's arms. Looking up at him and with the permission from her eyes, Hank kissed Jill's lips.

His fingertips explored her lean back, traveling up her spine and clutching her neck, resting her small head in his hands. Jill tried to resist the sexual desire flooding her body, but with every beat of her heart and every breath from her lungs, she pulled herself closer to him.

Like two teenagers, ignoring the other patrons at the bar, they continued to fondle each other's body through the parking lot until making it to Hank's truck. Stumbling like before, Hank helped Jill into his vehicle.

Fastening her safety belt, she asked, "Do you mind if we go back to your place. Mine is not fit for company." She didn't want Hank knowing she was staying with Rodgers.

Suggesting he fully intended on going to his place, he looked at Jill and winked. She trembled inside with anticipation.

"I have to ask, do you drive anything other then this Chevy?"

"This truck has been with me since I started college." Sensing she was uncomfortable with it ruggedness, Hank asked, "Did you expect me to drive a Porsche?"

"I don't know what I expected you to drive. I guess I am just surprised you drove this." Jill figured it was the alcohol furnishing the courage behind her questions. The way she referred to the truck was a little rude.

"I know she looks like she's barely holding on, but she has some good years left in her."

After driving only a few minutes, the green Chevy parked in front of beautiful Cathedral style home. There was scaffolding on the sides and drop cloths covered the doorstep and paint buckets, empty and full, scattered over the yard. It was obvious the building was going through some major renovations. A red brick wall, only a few feet high, fenced in the structure. The walk leading to the building was made from light tile, cut in all different patterns and shades. Four windows designed in an even pattern, cut from the wall and arched with thick windowsills. A single room third floor was decorated by clear glass, circling all around. A faint light emitted from the tower, looking like a familiar storybook castle.

Jill turned to Hank with curiosity.

Getting out of the pick-up without a word, he went to Jill's side of the truck, opened the door and kissed her again.

"Come on, I want to show you something."

She grabbed his hand and followed him up the walk.

Carefully stepping over the drop cloths, Jill could see in one of the finely crafted windows. A masterpiece of architecture rested neatly on the other side. The surroundings nudged her memory, had she been there?

Waiting for Hank to open the door, she searched her thoughts, trying to place the setting from her past. Once the door opened and the light switch was thrown, she lost the urge to remember. The sight of the spectacular construction confused her senses and she soaked in the décor.

Just beyond the entry, dividing the first floor stood a wide staircase. With only the slightest spiral, the stairs extended into the high ceiling. The building was empty, but the floors were made of the shiniest wood, almost glistening. A blanket of silk fell across the tops of all the windows. Each wall cast a light shade of rust swirled into a beige tone. Jill was enamored by the color of paint.

"This was an old clinic and pharmacy built in the mid 1800's. The state had never made it a historical building, so when it came up for auction, the price was right."

Jill now realized she was standing in the same home she had visited almost six years ago. Tucker had taken her to the very spot with dreams of turning the structure into the original pharmacy it had once been. Although the renovations were modern, the building still stood as it did back then. A local historical group owned it and the building came up for sale on a private market. When Tucker had attempted to make an offer, he was rejected. The clinic unexpectedly became tied up in litigation, something to do with the rightful owner. When Tucker found out it wasn't for sale, he never mentioned it again.

Jill wasn't going to explain the coincidence of the two of them being at the place she and Tucker had visited several years prior or ponder it any longer than the second that had already past. It had nothing to do with fate. Hank was obviously an artistic man. It was no surprise that he liked architect with history.

"Jill? Jill?" Hank tried to get Jill's attention, but she appeared to be caught in a daydream. Realizing his calls were useless, He circled around her, swallowing her up in his arms.

The touch brought her back to reality. "I'm sorry."

Looking up at a gorgeous chandelier, hanging in the center walkway, she moved towards it as if to get a better look. She enjoyed Hank's affection, but it was becoming an uninvited redundancy, a simple pleasure, but an intrusion as well.

As she followed him up the wide stairway, Jill wished her memory wasn't so vivid. It was like she was back, scoping the building for the first time. Even the generic tour rolled in the same order she and Tucker had walked. Hank's description of the changes, the progress and the possibilities of the clinic were all once similar aspirations of Tucker. At times, Jill felt a small urge to call Hank by Tucker's name.

Upstairs was a long hallway, six rooms, three on each side, all with large white doors. The walls were the same shade as the ones downstairs, only now there was a slender slab of molding, horizontal three feet from the floor, running the entire length of the hall.

Fashionably located at the end of the foyer, was the bathroom. Equipped with the modern day luxuries, Jill wondered how anyone ever survived with only one. It amazed her how people of earlier generations were so humble and meek. Even as a single woman and considerably modest, there were two restrooms in her apartment.

"What do you plan to do with this building once you finished remodeling?"

"I'm going to turn the downstairs into my private practice and the upstairs into my home. I have a great contractor and he believes he can make it quite livable up here. This small room adjacent to the lavatory is going to be the kitchen." Hank pointed to the bedroom. "I've already bought the appliances; I'm just waiting on the contractor to make the space."

"Wait," interrupting, "private practice?" Jill looked confused.

"Come spring, I am no longer going to work as a public defender. I am going to practice civil law. A lawyer friend of mine is going to share the office. A sign out front will read, *O'Donnell and Merger – Attorneys at Law*." As he spoke his hands waved in front of his face, similar to a Broadway musical number.

"Michael Merger has been a civil attorney for the last eight years. There is so much more money in civil litigation, I couldn't resist the switch. I need more cash," pausing briefly, "you know, to buy that Porsche." He finished with a wink.

Surprised by the news, she didn't press him for any more information than he was willing to give. Hank had been one of the top public defenders in Lubbock County and she knew he would be hard to replace. That was how it seemed to play out. If an attorney was worth anything at his trade, he tended to go where the money was and leave the rest behind.

Saying no more, he escorted her to a terrace off the north bedroom. The strong floor of the enchanted plank, which Hank called the balcony, was topped with burnt orange tile and trimmed with smaller rustic red brick. The pillars that enclosed the finely constructed alcove were a deep red wood, giving off a plentiful scent of cedar. It was lovely and romantic, but new. Jill didn't recall the balcony the last time she had seen the home. The only decorative landscaping was a patio off the downstairs French doors. She remembered imaging the Twentieth century staff retreating to the rear of the pharmacy to catch a smoke or to relax before the sick returned. Jill placed her tiny hands on the railing and listened to Hank's recollection of the remodeling.

"This balcony was not here originally and is the most expensive addition to the home. I'm not poor by any means, but I thought my bank accounts were going to run dry over this deal." He shrugged his eyebrows and continued, "I can't wait to see the final project."

Was he bragging or making small talk? Either way, Jill didn't like where it was going.

"This is all beautiful." Turning her body towards his, she added, "I hate to rush your tour, but I need to get back." The alcohol was beginning to metabolize in her body and she was thinking clearer and fairly responsible. "I don't want some fool at the bar thinking my car is there for his disposal. There's no telling how many men are staggering drunk outside the doors." She touched his shoulder as she turned around to go back inside. "This night has gone well; let's end it on a high note."

Hank nodded his approval, thinking maybe she was bored with his plans. Deciding not to chance losing the opportunity to see her again, he followed her in.

She was right. The Fifth Seasons Bar tended to

attract a variety of people and now it was almost too late to invite her back to his place; sex was definitely out of the scenario. Besides, he had waited this long, what was one more night?

CHAPTER ELEVEN

J ILL LET HERSELF IN WITH AN EMERGENCY KEY HE had given her in the event she needed somewhere to retreat or somewhere to hide. Although technically, this evening didn't fit in the actual realm of an emergency, she had no intentions of waking him to let her inside; waking him at this hour would be problematic.

Rodgers appeared asleep and luckily her entrance had not disturbed him. She knew he had probably spent half the evening pacing the floor, waiting for her arrival. When she hadn't called to tell him it would be later than sooner, he most likely stirred in his own anger and worry.

Tiptoeing to her room, she whispered a breath of relief as she closed the bedroom door. Taking her clothes off, she saw her phone sitting on the nightstand. Halfway through the evening she realized she had forgotten it and now remembered placing it there to change shoes. The red light was flashing, which meant there were messages. Rodgers she supposed. Well, it didn't matter now. She was back and would have to deal with his parental wrath in the morning. Maybe he would be gone for duty before she woke. It might give him a chance to cool off. Who was she kidding? Rodgers was going to be there no matter what time she rolled out of bed.

Shedding the last sock off her foot, she pulled back the comforter and climbed beneath the sheets. She preferred to sleep naked, but in Rodgers' house she wasn't completely convinced that she wasn't on camera. She opted to stay in bra and panties.

Lying with her butt cheeks to the cold mattress,

she shivered and began to relive the night in her thoughts. Hank had tried to impress her and besides the showiness of his investment, Jill liked what she saw. The date had gone well. She was glad she had gone out again. She had taken pleasure in her capacity to flirt with the possibilities of a relationship. Single life was great, but romance could be fun.

It didn't take long and Jill was lying there thinking again about Tucker. Yearning for rest, Jill closed her eyes and tried to avoid the image of the newly remodeled pharmacy. She desperately fought the fantasy of her past life.

"He was an evil man and hid behind that gentle veneer, ugh," she groaned out loud.

Rolling over on her side, her legs pulled to her chest in a fetal position, she was saddened at her inability to let the past go. Tucker's simple ways had fooled her into falling for him, desperately loving him. Wounded beyond repair, she promised herself to never give anything to another man, no matter how much she loved him.

"I will never be hurt again." She thought.

Still fighting the chill under the blankets and the lights out with quiet surrounding her, Jill cried herself to sleep.

CHAPTER TWELVE

I N THE ROOM ACROSS THE HALL, RODGERS PUT his reading glasses down. He placed a marker in his favorite book, saving the page. Not that it was necessary; he had read the book many times before, memorized every chapter and almost every line. A story of a valiant knight caught in a love triangle with the woman he loved and the woman he was destined to rescue, a fictional romance with a masculine twist. A fan of mostly westerns, this book had a captivating quality that intrigued his metro side and beneficially soothed his rising anxiety, a folklore that mirrored his life.

Earlier that evening, when Jill hadn't called, he became agitated and worried. Then, while putting clean linens on her bed, he had found her phone on the bedside table. It was out of character for her to go anywhere without her phone, but he regretfully rushed her. Blaming himself, Rodgers knew he was not going to reach her tonight, but neither was the freak that had been harassing her. Maybe her forgetfulness was a moment of serenity from her unknown stalker. Understanding there was little he could do; Rodgers had grabbed a book, climbed in bed and waited for her return.

Rodgers envisioned her lying peacefully, probably with the comforter pulled tight under her arms and her soft skin rubbing lightly over the sheets. He pictured her drifting to sleep from the angelic pose, dreaming, probably about the man she met for drinks.

At any point he could come up with some lame reason to go into the room and look at her, but he didn't. Rodgers lusted over many women but Jill he grew to respect. She was different. Jill was strong and independent. Jill didn't need a man; he only prayed she wanted one.

Pulling the table-lamp string, he fluffed his pillow and laid down his head. He closed his eyes. Rodgers could sleep now.

She was home.

CHAPTER THIRTEEN

THE SIGHT OF HER HEAD CONTENTLY NESTLED IN her hand, leaning and listening to every word. Her body hunched over the table, hiding the electrifying body she possessed. Her fingers wrapped around her glass with elegance. Her feet slightly crossed at the ankles, wiggling gently. Jill Holland was perfect in all sense of the word.

He enjoyed watching her eyes follow people around the bar, studying each one, genuinely intrigued. He found himself watching her the same way.

The trick of getting to know Jill began several years before. College was in session and the collegiate packs created long lines everywhere he went, waiting earnestly even to get a simple cup of coffee. But, on that particular day he didn't mind.

At a picturesque Coffee House, cozied up on a ragged sofa, taking advantage of the wireless internet and sipping on a cup of hot Topeka House choice of the day, immersed in the quiet, his attention was diverted to the jingle of the bell that had been sloppily tied to the front entrance. The last thing he expected was to be swept off his feet

Walking in with her duffle bag slung over her shoulder, blending with the college crew, she stylishly filled the room with joy. She was not alone. There was an older man, attractive enough, possibly a professor. He never guessed they were a romantic couple until the man kissed her with so much passion that the fact was unmistakable. The two were in love. It was obvious in their affection and the way the man made her laugh and the way she made him smile, mesmerized by one another. It was the kind of fondness that every person wished for, something that stays with you, even if you are just watching from afar. He didn't know her name then, but never forgot her face.

Days later, he had seen her again, walking into the World Market on 4th Street, resting her arms on the cart handle with one foot propped up on the bottom of the basket. Lost in her own shopping list, never noticing him.

With its assortment of organic and worldly selections, the store attracted the younger, fit crowd. He too kept his body in check, working out regularly and stocking up on protein bars and non-fat yogurt. Sometimes he treated himself to a pint of wheat grass, but only if he was scheduled to run during his Cross-Fit Routine. He shopped at the World Market and frequented the store more when he learned she shopped there too.

Later that year, he saw her jogging at the Bothom Park on University Street. Loaded with swings and slides and the celebrated sea-saws, the park had an inviting appeal, providing refuge for families and kids. A one mile black top path enclosed the wonderland, adding to the allure for the physically fit.

It was chilly then and he was wearing a hoodie and pants. People of all ages crowded the path, some walking, and others running, each adorned in winter ware. Jill was draped with a cotton sweatshirt and matching sweats. He remembered the sweet smell of her perfume as he passed her on a loop. His hood drawn close to his ears and gloves clinging tight to his hands, he knew she hadn't seen him, but he definitely saw her.

The accidental encounters became regular and he given himself wanting more and more, a suited game for him. Like an addict, craving the chase of her shadow. He fought the addiction, but gave in with little regret. She was easy to be devilish for.

He could not believe that life had brought something so special to him. A woman like Jill was few and far between. He hadn't been looking for her when she appeared, but never stopped expecting her to find him. And she did.

Now with only a sheet of glass and sheer curtains between him and his love, he prepared himself for their next encounter. Watching her cry, he knew it would have to be soon. She needed him. A stealth voyeur, caressing her soft naked flesh in his mind, unleashing his sexual fantasies and watching her body weep at a short distance. Obeying his heart, he knew it was time to introduce himself, especially before the detective got in his way again. Or better yet, before Jill realized the detective had fallen too.

CHAPTER FOURTEEN

THE SMELL OF FRESH COFFEE BREWING LURED Jill to wake up. Rodgers was a big coffee lover. He had several flavors stashed away in his freezer for the rear occasions of sleep over guests. .

Standing, she quickly reached for her robe at the end of the bed. The room and floors were bitter cold. She hated that she didn't pack slippers. Wrapping the belt tightly around her small waist, opening the bedroom door, she walked towards the kitchen.

Jill noticed the clock on the microwave, quarter to seven. "God it's early."

"Good morning to you too." His voice echoed into the kitchen. Rodgers had been in the utility room finding a clean shirt when he heard Jill shuffle in.

"There's a fresh pot of coffee on. Would you like anything to eat?" He could be hospitable from time to time; especially if a good looking woman was visiting.

Rubbing her eyes, she cleared them of morning dew, suggesting proof of her late night tears. Opening cabinet doors, she was unsuccessful in her search for clean dishes.

"Where are your coffee mugs?"

"Check the dishwasher."

Like most bachelors, Rodgers waited for the last dish to dirty before he washed anything. When he did, he used the dishwasher as storage.

"How was your night?"

Jill anticipated a morning lecture. Walking in the kitchen, he pleaded, "Wait, before you answer, I called you a few times and then realized you didn't have your phone. So when you listen to your voicemails or if you have listened to them, just know all I could think about last night was the perp. I'm sorry." Rodgers feared she was less then thrilled with his intentions.

"I noticed there were messages and yes, I did have a good time last night. He was a gentleman, or at least more of a gentleman than I've been out with lately." Which was not entirely true, she had been to dinner with Rodgers, but she wouldn't begin to call that a date.

"Kid, I'm worried about you. This guy's shown he is not afraid to get close to you. He is watching where you are going and whom you are with. He was brazen enough to go to your house."

Jill interrupted, "if that's even the same person".

"Seriously Jill, are you that naive?" Rodgers' voice spoke volumes. He only called her by name when he wanted to drive home a point. This was one she needed to get.

Jill sat down the coffee cup she was rising clean from the dishwasher.

"Do you think I don't know that this could become dangerous fast? Hell Rodgers, give me a break. I agreed to stay here, but I didn't agree to be babysat." Picking up a cloth off the counter, she wiped dry the mug and filled it full of coffee. The steam from the cup calmed her.

"You deserve a little peace in your life, kid. I wish for once you would let someone carry you instead of you trying to do it all."

"Then carry me, but don't lecture me." She demanded while sipping the hot coffee.

An uncomfortable silence fell across the room.

Rodgers snapped the last button on his shirt and turned away. She sensed her words had hurt him. She knew Rodgers meant well, but not everyone was Tucker Stiles. Then at that moment, she realized the truth of her own words.

Fighting the impulse, Jill found herself following him into the bedroom. There he stood, stringing his tie around his neck, fumbling with the material, making a mess of the bow. Jill walked to him and pushed his hands out of the way. Like a magic trick, she tied it like men would for Sunday service.

Patting his chest and turning back towards the door, Jill uttered, "I just don't get you." She continued to talk as she walked away, "your first impression is demeaning, shallow, and selfish. You make me sick with your condescending, chauvinistic slang. Then you invite me into your life; show me that there is a gentleman underneath the hard shell and good looks." Jill could feel her face blush. "Now in a moment of weakness, you make me feel guilty for not liking you."

Glancing back, the two smiled at each other. Rodgers took it as an apology and Jill meant it as one.

The only person who knew Jill like the back of their hand was Rodgers. For the last five years he had seen her shine and over the last five years had seen her fall. He was her net, her umbrella when the storms came crashing down. He was the light that kept the boogieman away and the shield that warded off pain.

Considering herself as a strong modern day Mary Taylor Moore, too independent to let a man carry her load, knowing she could do it all, Jill found it hard to let anyone carry her burdens. But there was something

Rodgers offered that she hadn't found in any other man and hadn't expected to find in him, safety. Even though his words were gruff and irritating at times, she made room for him in her life and had learned to care for him and hesitantly accepted his security.

Making her way back to the kitchen, pulling the creamer from the refrigerator, she heard Rodgers return too.

"I guess your car is parked outside?" He opened the blinds. Jill's vehicle was parked parallel to his.

The question was meant rhetorical, but Jill answered with a bit of sarcasm. "Oh yea, I wasn't going to have Hank give me a ride back to your place."

"Hank? Hank O'Donnell, the lawyer?"

Jill nodded, taking another drink of coffee.

"Jill," sighing, he continued, "He's shady and not to mention, on the other side."

Jill didn't get that with cops, other side? Did they expect lawyers to play favorites because they were part of the judicial system? She proclaimed that if the police did their jobs correctly, fairly and professionally, the lawyers wouldn't be on anyone's side and the criminals would be going to jail.

"Actually, he is going into private practice. Public defending does not strike his interest anymore. So, he will be on the peoples' side, if there even is a side." Jill was becoming more sarcastic.

Rodgers shook his head and grabbed his keys and gun.

"What?" Jill asked with a malicious smile.

"Be careful and call me if you need anything." He

spoke frank as he slid his weapon in his side holster hidden behind his coat. He waved good-bye.

Jill could feel the wrath of winter sneak inside as Rodgers opened the door. A cold breeze tickled her toes. Curling them and moving out of winter's path, she again wished she had brought her slippers.

Before the door closed, she could smell and hear a slow steady rain falling. It was the kind of winter storm she wished she could watch snuggled under a fluffy comforter, reading a good book, drinking a mug of warm hot chocolate. Unfortunately, like most mornings, winter storm or not, she had work to do. The book would have to wait.

From the kitchen window, she watched Rodgers put on his seatbelt and report for duty from his in car radio. Jill wondered what that was like, checking in with dispatch every day, notifying some stranger every time your agenda changed. She was fortunate with Jared. Jill was usually the one he reported to.

Catching her gawking, Rodgers threw her a wave and disappeared into traffic.

Waving back and moving from the window, Jill started her day.

CHAPTER FIFTEEN

KNOWING THAT SHE WOULD BE HELD CAPTIVE until some kind of lead into her own affairs, she brought plenty of work to keep her mind occupied. She planned to update a case set for grand jury and return messages that had begun to collect dust. But first, she needed to get dressed.

Pulling her bulky bag from the floor, she laid it on a bench at the end of the bed. The brown paisley print on her bag put flavor in the badly decorated room. Jill knew Rodgers was not responsible for the room décor. No man was capable of splattering one color so thick throughout a room and making it work, that was reminisce of Jaclyn.

Several shades of blue were dispersed all around the room including the window treatments. Blue curtains hung from the tops of the ceiling, dragging their seam on the blue and white plumped pillows tossed on the window seat. The rug, slightly off center in front of the seat was a baby blue, something that a new parent would add to a newborns nursery. In the corner, to the left of the window seat, was a white six drawer antique dresser, adorned with blue and white handles, the same shade of blue as the rug. A sheer blue lampshade with a white base sat on top the dresser. Jill could see a white doily peeking out from the bottom, probably put there to protect the furniture. The two nightstands were the only obvious pieces of furniture without the touches of blue. Even the headboard of the bed was decorated with a blue rose flowered swag.

Rummaging through her suitcase for something comfortable to wear, she noticed her cell phone was still blinking, reminding her she still hadn't listen to her messages. Dialing voice mail she knew she was going to be irritated by Rodgers repetitive pleas for her to call. She was right. With the phone placed slightly against her ear, she furiously listened to each voicemail.

The first recording had no words, just Rodgers scrambling with the buttons on his cell to hang up. She couldn't help but laugh to herself. She remembered the day he bought the tiny contemporary phone. It was another poor attempt by Rodgers to keep up with modern technology. He was so excited, but still needed her to show him how to turn it on.

The messages continued. Jill counted four. Each one was deleted before she listened to it completely. Her temper was quickly rising. Rodgers had a tendency to be annoying when her patience was at it lowest. She was not going to check in with Rodgers no matter how concerned he was, ever.

Jill thought she had listened to the last one, but the recorded voice of the world-renowned voice mail lady stated that one new message was not heard. Jill pushed the one key to listen.

. A bright flash of lightening filled the room and a howling crush of thunder soon followed. Losing her breath and slumping to the floor, she recognized the man's voice as the same one that called her after lunch with Melissa. Leaning against the bed with her legs exposed from the robe; she listened scarily to his words.

"You looked beautiful, your hair perfectly done and your eyes looking to everyone, catching every stare. You were shinning in the bar. What was that perfume you

were wearing? It smelt good on your skin. You don't know what you do to me, do you? Everything you do excites me. The way your body brushed up against mine made me tingle all over. This is the way it was meant to be. You were made for me, its destiny. I've known that since the first time I laid eyes on you, you remember? You were with Tucker. God, you were stunning. Even now as I see you standing there wearing nothing more than your bra and thong, I can't help but want you."

The voice took a long break, breathing heavy on the other end. *"I can't play this game anymore; I need you. I promise you will not be disappointed! "*

The voice broke again. *"You sleep well my princess, because tomorrow we meet. Sweet dreams."* Making a kissing sound into the phone, the man hung up and the message ended.

Pulling herself to her feet, she quickly looked around the room. Her hands were shaking uncontrollably.

"Oh my God," her breath was becoming short. "Rodgers I need you."

Dialing wrong on the first attempt, Jill tried to reach Rodgers. She had to fight her shake. She looked at the screen and discovered she had left out the first digit in his phone number. Trying again, she got a busy tone, as if the phone had no service.

"Shit!" She screamed as she tossed the phone on the bed. The fear was all too familiar to Jill. For the last five years she was trying to forget the monster she fell in love with and regretfully attracted another.

Shutting the bedroom door, she hastily walked to the window. She quickly pulled the curtains together, closing off any view someone might have inside the room that had quickly become her dungeon. She was locked up by the terror of what was outside waiting for her, trapped by another nightmare.

Her body plopped down on the bed, grabbing the phone off the sheets; she attempted to reach Rodgers again. This time she got his voice mail and told him it was an emergency, to come home as soon as he could.

Another bust of thunder shook the house, causing Jill to jump. She recognized her fear and grasped at sanity, she had to make a plan. Her first priority was to get dressed. Randomly pulling a top and bottom from her suitcase, she threw a shirt over her head. As quickly as she had put on the shirt, she put on a pair of pants. Covering her body made her feel minimally safer.

She started contemplating how much this person had been watching her. She remembered the letters left in her mail box, one in particular. This nut wanted to die with her never leaving her side or something of that nature. Her mind was mush. It all seemed to be running together. She just wanted it to go away, she wanted normalcy.

"I got to get out of this town." Jill cried to herself.

Slithering her fingers through her hair, she pulled it up in a ponytail, wrapping it secure with a rubber band from her bag. It was an unconscious move she usually did before she got down to business, a trademark recognized by her colleagues when she was about to bring out the fury and crush her opponent.

"Okay, Jill," she said out loud. "Who is always around that you haven't noticed?" She retrieved a notebook from her bag and a pen from her wallet. She began jotting down names of all those that could be suspects.

Like a good attorney she suspected everyone, Jared, Hank, even Rodgers. But one name stood out stronger than the others, Troy Scott. He was constantly at her heels in college and recently poked out of nowhere; around the same time this mess began.

She decided to call the local news stations and see if he was employed with any locally. Why did he stop trailing her at college? Was her no's enough or had it been a plan for this? These were questions that made her even more suspicious of his sudden reappearance.

"Alright, little lady, quit being a scaredy cat."

Truthfully, she wasn't. She came from a long line of strong people. She always kept herself from falling the minute she started to lean. At this moment, she would put her craft to work.

Jill couldn't fight this person from the bedroom. She would have to walk right into his trap, whatever it might be. She was tired of being scared and now she was mad. Reaching in her bag, she pulled out a 40-caliber pistol she had bought herself after her last love affair. She had gone through all the red tape, classes, wrote checks and was now a concealed handgun license carrier. The gun was usually at her side, wherever she went, now it was going to the kitchen with her.

Opening the door with caution, peeking around the edge, much like her father would have done, Jill saw it was safe. She moved to the kitchen where she remembered seeing the phone book. Pilfering through the pile of books and papers Rodgers had staked on the counter, she found a copy of the yellow pages. Before she turned to the broadcasting stations, she was startled by a knock at the front door.

Her blood began to sore through her body. Her palms began to sweat. Clinching hard to her gun she walked towards the door. Wincing at the possibility that the crazy man was on the other side, she slowly pushed her eye to the peephole. A sigh of relief emptied her lungs. Laying down her gun, she opened the door.

"Hank, I am so glad to see you."

"Is everything okay?" Hank grabbed her elbow with genuine concern and escorted her back into the house.

"Yeah," Jill turned around, throwing a paper over her weapon. She definitely didn't need Hank to think she had lost her mind.

"I found your wallet in my truck and wanted to get it back to you. I went by your office, but they said you were out today and that you were working here. Are you sure you are okay?" Hank saw the butt of the gun under the paper she had tried to hide. Trying not to divert his eyes in that direction, he suggested they sit down. Handing her the wallet, he followed her into the kitchen.

"I have been under a little stress. You know how the courts can be. Thank you for my wallet. To be honest, I hadn't even notice I was missing it." She felt her pockets of her pants. Looking down she realized she dressed poorly, green cargo pants and a small orange tank with green and purple dots. The combination was awful; even she couldn't pull it off.

"Wow, look at me. Give me a second to throw something on; I'll just be a minute. There's coffee made and mugs in the dishwasher, help yourself." She rushed back to the blue room, hoping she hadn't ruined the progress she had made with Hank by her panic attack wardrobe. Pulling out tan slacks and a white blouse, she took off the hideous tank, picking out brown sketchers at the same time. She looked at the mirror and straightened the shirt. She tied her shoes and felt more attractive then before.

It wasn't a minute later and she was back in the kitchen with Hank. He had taken her up on the invitation for coffee and was sitting at the table sipping from a comedic mug. Jill never understood why anyone would waste money on dinnerware that had words instead of designs. Rodgers tended to collect the more vulgar ones and Jill was embarrassed that Hank was drinking from one.

"I see you found the detective's good china." Jill raised her eyebrows and poured herself another cup.

"Gotta love cops." With a little giggle in his words, Hank laughed, "It is funny."

Hank had found a dishcloth on the counter and was wiping his arms and legs dry from the downpour of rain.

"I really had a good time last night." His body conveyed the proof of their late night. His eyes were heavy and his face was flushed.

"Me too."

"I came by this morning, one to return you wallet, but also because I had to see you again." Hank leaned over the table and laid his fingers gently over her hand.

Jill could feel her stomach flutter. She looked at him and his eyes pierced hers.

Hank stood up, never moving his hand; he guided her to her feet, pulling her hair out from the tightly bound band, letting her hair lay down her back, he softly kissed her lips. She opened her mouth slightly and let his tongue chase hers', warm saliva escaped from one mouth to another. He squeezed her body against his chest and she released a deep sigh, approval that he could take her.

Jill let her hands coast the side of his body, chiseling the form with an imaginary tool, sliding easily from the winter wet caused from the storm. Each muscle feeling like it was going to break from the skin. He was her Michael Angelo come to life. Their two bodies traveled to the bedroom as one sexual explosive, near detonation.

Moving her bag out of the way, Hank tossed her on the bed. He took off her shoes, then her pants. Slowly moving up her body, he stopped briefly to kiss her inner thigh. Jill arched her back reaching for his shoulders and pulling him on top of her. Their bodies continued to move over one another, friction building between their soft skins. Never loosing touch, Jill lost all self-respect and gave herself to him. Hank caressed Jill's body until her sexual bomb exploded, again and again.

Jill's fears were no more. The stalker was gone from her thoughts. For the first time in years, Jill was at peace and fell asleep.

CHAPTER SIXTEEN

INTO THE AFTERNOON, THEY LAY EXHAUSTED ON the bed, close, as if they had been together forever. Hank carefully pulled his arm out from under her neck, waking her. Jill rolled over and looked deep into his eyes, questioning his thoughts.

"I wondered what this would be like, holding you, loving you." Hank drew his hand down her cheek as he spoke.

Jill was surprised at his choice of words, deep and intense. Smiling back, she closed her eyes and kissed him again.

"I want to be with you forever. Tell me this will never end, we'll never end, its destiny."

Jill froze. Those words. The letters. Opening her eyes she could feel a sudden sweat build between her fingers. She felt like she was standing on the edge of a skyscraper, anticipating a fall.

Looking at Hank she knew.

Trying to get out of bed, Hank yanked her back towards him.

"Wait; tell me this didn't feel right? I knew the moment I saw you that you belonged to me."

Jill couldn't believe she missed it. Of course it was Hank. The reference to the bar, no one had touched her but him. He was the only one who got close enough to smell her perfume on her skin.

She hadn't told anyone at the office where she was working. Rodgers had insisted that, he knew no one could be trusted. Hank had clearly followed her after their date. He had watched her undress and probably seen her cry herself to sleep.

"Oh my god," she cried.

And the re-modeled house, it wasn't coincidence; he was the buyer when Tucker had considered purchasing the property. She remembered now that it was an attorney named Merger was investigating the ownership of the property, the same name Hank gave as the lawyer joining his practice.

"How long have you been watching me?" She teared up thinking about her privacy and the things he might have seen. How long had this been going on and how far was he really ready to go? Had he just gotten brave enough to approach her or had she just let her guard down to accept another man's sinful companionship?

"I haven't been watching you. I've been studying you." He spoke with disappointment. "I wanted to know what made you smile, what you liked, so I could do that for you, make you happy." Hank was not convinced that he was doing anything wrong. He truly believed he was meant to be with her and that his crazy actions were acceptable because of that.

She tore herself away from him and began to put her clothes back on. He stood, his naked body in front of her, reminding her of the grave mistake she had made.

"Get out." Jill picked up Hank's clothes and hurled them in his direction. "You're crazy!"

She had gained a sense of security over the years. Despite the fear of him hurting her physically, she was not about to fall into a tug of war with her emotions.

"I told you Jill, I don't want to live without you. I'm not like Tucker. I won't go out without you." Hank dropped his clothes and moved closer to her.

"Stop! Don't come any closer."

"Jill, I don't want to hurt you. I know about your past. I want to complete your life. I want to make it better. Please, just listen to me." He stated to sound desperate.

"You have run away from me since the first day I saw you. Please, we are special, you and I. Give me a chance." Hank didn't wait for her to answer. He walked over to where she was standing and gripped her arms, descending his lips to hers.

Jill jerked away. As she turned, she felt a dirtiness fall over her. She had let another man in her life and he proven her argument that they were all sick and selfish.

Hank walked away too. Defeated he put his clothes back on.

"I thought you were different."

Jill refused to respond. He had followed her for who knows how long and then taken advantage of her vulnerability. She despised him.

"I was hoping it wouldn't come to this. I want you to know, Rodgers isn't coming for you."

Jill faced him. Her eyes gave away her terror.

"That's right. Let's just say he is a little tired and bruised with having to tend to you and your, stalker." Using his fingers, Hank made quotation marks in the air.

"He came by to see me this morning; it seems he knew I was responsible for the calls and letters. I give him credit. He's good. Evidently, I asked about you last week, said I hoped he could keep you safe as always. My interests made him question my involvement. I guess I gave myself away. Knowing he would not be returning home, it was a perfect time to introduce my love to you."

"What have you done?" Annunciating, Jill finished, "Who are you?"

"I'm your someday." His tone turned from evil to adoring. "The only man in your life who really knows what you need. A man not looking for just a few one night stands, but one who is there for you."

Hank turned as if he was leaving the room. Then with no warning, he leaped over the bed, knocking Jill to the ground.

Lying on top of her he told her, "I love you and I am going to spend the rest of my life proving it to you."

Jill pleaded with him, "Hank, please."

Wiggling away from his kisses, she managed to push her body up the wall until she was on her feet.

"Don't fight it Jill. You are here with me and I intend to keep it that way."

Something in Jill snapped and before she knew it, bumping against the dresser, she reached up for the small lamp. In one quick motion, she flung it over her head and down on Hank's. Startled, he fell to the floor. Jill ran to the door. Never looking back, she went for her gun.

Making it to the living room, she lifted the paper covering her pistol.

"What?" She began to panic.

"I thought you might go for that."

She spun around to see Hank holding the gun at his side.

"I retrieved it while you were sleeping. Good lawyers prepare."

She stepped aside, fearing his next move.

"Now what, you going to shoot me? Well, do it. There is no way in hell that I am going to let another psycho in my life. All I wanted was a friend, a lover, but you are crazy. God knows what you did to Rodgers." Jill began to cry.

"Jill," Hank went to her to hold her. In his demented mind he thought he could help.

For a brief moment of self-pity, Jill let him put his arms around her. It was crazy, but it allowed her time to think. She cried into his shoulder, gathering her thoughts and planning a diversion, Rodgers wasn't coming for her this time.

She had walked into this mess regrettably with her eyes closed. Now her time was running out. It was vital she act quickly. Lifting her foot off the ground with intense force, she shrewdly positioned her knee under his crotch, dropping him in a panting whimper.

Jill threw herself towards the kitchen, attempting to escape out the utility room back door, but just before she got free, she felt the frightening hand wrap around her ankle. Loosing her step, she fell to the hard wood floor. Crippling pain shot to her elbow, using it to catch her fall.

Hank pulled her back. Now with their bodies again side by side, Jill could see the insanity swimming in his eyes. In a flash she recalled the messages on her phone. The man on the line, she had heard him before. The voice, she remembered the man from college. It was Hank, smaller then, but still the same man. She had seen him around, at the store, on her runs, even at the cemetery when she would visit her dad, but he was never alone. Troy Scott was usually right behind him. Until now, she had not put the two together.

"You remember me don't you?"

"Its you." She had much more to say, but no energy to say it with.

Jill lay still waiting for an explanation, sorting through the realization that Hank had followed her since before law school. He probably knew her every move, but why had he decided to act now and what was his connection to Troy?

"At first it was a dream, then a game." As Hank spoke he stroked her hair, looking back and forth from her eyes to her lips, craving another kiss.

"I tried to forget you, but I couldn't. You were everywhere. Troy wouldn't give me an opportunity to talk to you. He was always right there, right when I was about to introduce myself. When I went to work as a public defender, Troy thought I had taken it too far. That bastard kicked me out of the apartment, so I had to find you myself, without his help. It was hard work and a little intimidating. I put off our introduction as long as I could."

Hanks eyes began to water, tears rested in the corners. Jill almost believed he was hurting.

"When the paper covered the story about Tucker and the way you had to fight for your life, I knew you needed me."

Jill was starting to put the puzzle together.

"Troy was my roommate. He only continued to ask you out to distract you from me. He told me it was dangerous, the fascination I had for you. Your pictures were all over my wall, a shrine; Troy said only criminals kept shrines. I'd laugh and then we would drink a beer. I needed him around, to keep me close to you."

A short silence followed.

"You deserved peace and I wanted to give that to you. I had to find you. In some sick way, I became scared of you; afraid you would turn me down. So, I waited and sent you letters. That older woman who lives behind you stole some of them. I think she was playing a game too. When I saw her take them, I figured you hadn't gotten any, so I decided to ask you out, tell you in person how I felt. I wasn't that poetic anyway. "Your friend Rodgers made it hard to stay on track. He kept getting in the way, stepping in front of my gestures." Hank gripped a handful of hair on the back of her hair, slamming her lips to his. He couldn't fight the craving anymore.

Jill was not going to let this happen. Brushing her thigh against the gun, she realized he had dropped it when she damaged his manhood.

"You're not thinking about getting that are you?" Hank sensed her next move and seemed to be ready.

"You got me where you want me." Jill caressed his face, holding his cheek in her hand. She had learned that the only way to beat a crazy person was to join them. "Teach me how to play, show me what to do." Little to his knowledge, she planned on teaching him.

Hank rolled on top of her, putting his arms above her head and kissing her passionately. Faking the passion and returning the kiss, she dragged her nails softly down his back and continued down his arms.

Never shutting her eyes, she anticipated Hank to open his and know that she was going for the gun. He didn't. Exchanging saliva, she was able to convince him her kisses were with sincerity and in one quick move; she had her hands around the gun. Familiar with the weapon, she dropped the magazine, making it useless against her.

Hank opened his eyes and rage came over him. Pulling the gun from her hand, and using the tip of the barrel, he slapped her against the face. Jill was oblivious to the pain; her only objective was to break free.

Scrambling to her knees, she gave the magazine a shove and it went flying across the room. Crawling to the coffee table, Jill was able to put some distance between them.

Knowing the weapon was useless; Hank tossed it on the couch, paying no attention to where it landed.

"Jill, you deserve the best, a man who comes home to you each night wanting to be by your side, no expectations." Hank began rubbing his forehead in a desperate attempt to figure out his next persuasion. "I will defer only to a man that loves you more than me."

Before Hank could say another word Jill saw Rodgers stagger into the doorway.

"Then defer to me." In a tired, beaten voice, Rodgers struggled to hold himself up, wiping blood from his neck as he aimed a shotgun in Hank's direction.

Jill screamed, placing her hands over her mouth, muffling her terror.

Hank turned for the pistol. Realizing he had thrown it out of sight, he turned back to Rodgers and faced his death.

"You should have died where I left you."

"Funny," pausing only to cough, "you attorney's always underestimate us cops. We have bodies of steel and undying wills. You sir left before the fight was over."

Without a blink, Rodgers chambered a slug in the barrel. The sound sent fear crawling up Jill's spine. The end was inevitable. Within seconds, Rodgers had pulled the trigger and Hank fell to the floor.

Collapsing to his knees and falling to the floor, Rodgers called for Jill.

Already running to him, she ignored the lifeless body that lie on the other side of the room. Kneeling beside Rodgers, she witnessed the brutality of Hank's madness. Picking up his shoulders and resting them in her hands, feeling his weight pull her closer to the floor, she pleaded with him to stay awake.

"Oh my god, what did he do to you?" Jill wiped the blood from Rodgers head and ears. He was badly hurt and she desperately tried to believe he was going to live.

"Jill, I called for back up, they should be here soon." Rodger's voice was quite, almost a whisper. His eyes were heavy, straining to keep them open.

Jill could hear the sirens as he struggled to speak. "Rodgers hang on, help is coming, and they're almost here." She was crying again, dropping tears on his cheek. "Hang on Rodgers, I need you."

Dropping her chin to her chest, trounced and tired, she felt his hand slowly lift to her cheek. Looking into his defeated eyes, she desired so much more time.

Coughing briefly, Rodgers managed to say, "You don't need me. You can let go now, Jill."

"Rodgers, please, I do need you!" Jill was not going to let him go. Holding tight to his body she began to cry hard. The same cry she cried when her father and grandfather died and the same cry when she lost Tucker.

With a slight whisper, Rodgers asked, "Do you love me?" He seemed a bit stronger now, like the anticipation of her answer gave him life.

"I ..."

Jill knew the risks, but she did love him. She knew she was loosing him and he needed to know the truth. Nodding her answer, she made it clear.

"I love you."

With those words and the assurance of her tears, Rodgers left the world knowing she loved him too.

CHAPTER SEVENTEEN

JILL JUST SAT ON THE POUCH. THE SUN WAS SETTING behind the dark gray storm clouds. The ambulance and corners office had came and gone. A few officers were still walking around trying to piece together the tragic picture that she had come to know as her life.

The crime scene tape flapped against the wet ground, paying no attention to its true purpose and waving in the wind with no regard. The porch swing creaked as the cold winter wind blew. Swathed in a bright yellow emergency blanket, sitting on the top step, Jill believed her world was losing ground, once again.

The officer who took the initial report had come to the scene. Watching him work his way to her position, Jill wondered if he did everything to protect her and to save Rodgers. Did he follow through on his leads? Did he have any leads? Did he discuss with Rodgers the possible suspects? Did he suspect Hank too?

Patting her shoulder and walking into the house, the officer said nothing. Jill said nothing. There was nothing to say.

Looking at the sky to shout words to her God, to tell him she was done playing, her words were silenced. A ghost from her past emerged. Holding a production size camera, Troy Scott, the man that let the monster roam free, was standing in front of her.

"I'm sorry," putting the camera down on the only dry spot on the concrete, he added, "I thought it was over. I never thought he would take it this far."

"Why didn't you tell me? Why didn't you tell the police?" Jill only shook her head, never raising her voice; never making any gesture that she accepted his apology. "You are responsible for my newest nightmare. You are the one who has the blood of the man I loved on your hands. You were directly involved, attached, linked and you did nothing. I blame you." Jill spoke the words slow and precise. She was not angered and not sad, just matter a fact.

Picking up his camera, Troy walked away, looking back only once, never losing step.

As Jill sat motionless, she pondered the choices she had made in her life. Being an educated woman, she ironically never really had a good understanding of men. When it came to the opposite sex, she was emotionally immature, not yet grown in her ability to pick the strong, faithful and sane one. It became her way.

Looking at the darkness that was rising from the horizon, and the sun that was hiding from the moon, Jill realized that despite her choices, a few great men had surrounded her. She may have overlooked their efforts to love her, but she never overlooked their ability to teach her and those teachings would be what would carry her now.

Her father had taught her to be strong and not lose sight in what she was aiming for. He reminded her that it was her inner core that carried the load and she needed to "explore the possibilities of cracking through the hard stuff". His words were still loud and clear.

Her grandfather taught love and generosity, giving her the blessing of faith. Even in the end, he held her hand and told her life was a gift, to treat it kindly.

And Rodgers had given her permission to trust

herself and to fight against everything when nothing was fighting for her. He would tell her that she could turn to herself when no one else seemed to be on her side, and if she didn't, he would jokingly remind her that he would be there to catch her, rain or shine. Today he proved to her that he was there and like her father and grandfather, Rodgers would be pulling for her from Heaven.

Sitting alone, blurring out the background of the cops and emergency vehicles that surrounded Rodgers' home, Jill understood she was her own protector now and that tomorrow would be a new day. And just like the times before, she would be okay, she always was.